I0553904

CHOPPER COPS
SKY WAR

CALIBER
BOOKS

Also from MICHAEL KASNER

BLACK OPS Series

BLACK OPS: Undercover War
BLACK OPS: Armageddon Now
BLACK OPS: Deep Cover

WARKEEP 2030 Series

WARKEEP 2030: Black Gold
WARKEEP 2030: Killing Fields
WARKEEP 2030: Jungle Breakout
WARKEEP 2030: Finger of God

CHOPPER COPS Series

CHOPPER COPS: Northwest Inferno
CHOPPER COPS: Gulf Attack
CHOPPER COPS: Recon Strike Force
CHOPPER COPS: Sky War

CHOPPER COPS: SKY WAR

For further information visit the Caliber Comics website:
www.calibercomics.com

CHAPTER 1

The city of Reno had pulled out all the stops for the first airshow of the new millennium. The newest of NASA's space shuttles, the Enterprise II, was open for public viewing as was the prototype of Boeing's hypersonic Orient Express transport due to go into service later that year. Examples of the Northrup F-23 Scorpion advanced tactical fighter, the old Lockheed F-117 stealth fighter and the new Grumman A-12 Avenger attack plane were lined up on the tarmac next to examples of the Soviet Union's latest hardware. Three of the bat-wing B-2 stealth bombers had put on a demonstration earlier that morning and a flight of the vertical takeoff V-22 Osprey assault gunships had been put through their paces.

As popular as the modern, hi-tech aircraft were, however, the real crowd pleasers were still the classic World War Two War birds, the heroes of the last real air war. The Army Air Force veterans of WW II, the B-17 Flying Fortresses, the B-24 Liberators, and the P-51 Mustangs had already had their turn in the air and now the Navy veterans of the Pacific war were taking their turn.

A dark navy-blue Corsair screamed over the runway only

fifty feet above the tarmac before gracefully banking up on one wing tip and rocketing back up into the china-blue desert sky. The thunder of its 2,300 horsepower Pratt and Whitney radial engine battered the ears of the spectators and the hurricane generated by its massive, four-bladed prop brought tears to their eyes.

The gull-winged F4U-5 Corsair was one of the most powerful piston-engine fighters ever built, and the pilot was putting his restored war bird through its paces to the delight of the airshow crowd. Even in an age of exotic, mach two, stealth aircraft, the thundering old Navy fighter stirred the emotions in a way that no modern plane could. The sun glinted off the plane's polished gull wings as the Corsair reached the top of its climb and the pilot kicked the fighter over into a hammerhead stall to dive back down on the crowd.

In the aircraft static display area, two men in dark-blue police flight suits with bright-yellow neck scarves and colorful patches on the breasts of their uniforms watched as the diving Corsair pulled up a few feet off the ground and screamed across the runway again, the tips of its four-bladed prop almost touching the ground.

"He's really flogging it today." The muscular black with the bushy mustache and shaved head smiled as he watched the Corsair pilot pull up into an Immelmann turn at the end of the runway.

Tactical Police Force Sergeant Jumal "Mojo" Mugabe usually flew the gunner's seat in a TPF Griffin helicopter with the Corsair's pilot, fellow TPF Lieutenant Rick Wolff. Today, however, he and TPF Sergeant Daryl "Gunner" Jennings were on hand with a Tac Force Dragon Flight Griffin to give the public their first chance to see one of the potent police gunships up close.

The Bell 506P Griffin was the first helicopter designed specifically for police work. Using state-of-the-art military technology, the Griffin was a combination of high-tech gunship, airborne surveillance ship, and aerial patrol car.

Two small but powerful 750 shaft horsepower General Electric turbines pod mounted externally on the fuselage powered the Griffin, driving a four-bladed, forty-foot diameter rigid rotor. Both the main rotor and the shrouded tail rotor had been designed for noise suppression as well as maximum maneuverability.

While not primarily a gunship, the Griffin was capable of being armed with a variety of weapons in its nose turret and on the stub wing weapons pylons. Normally, a 40mm grenade launcher was fitted to the 360-degree turret along with a select fire, 25mm chain gun. Along with the weapons, the ship was armored to withstand ground fire up to 7.62mm armor-piercing ammunition. Self-sealing fuel tanks, armored nacelles for the turbines, an armored crew compartment with a bullet proof Lexan canopy and Kevlar seats insured that the Griffin could take it as well as dish it out.

The heart of the Griffin, however, was in its sophisticated sensors and communications systems. Using either the active infrared or light-intensifying system, the Griffin could see in the dark. Working in conjunction with terrain-following radar navigation and mapping system, this allowed the pilot to know where he was at all times, day or night. Three types of radar—infrared imaging, all-frequency electromagnetic radiation detectors, and audiovisual taping systems completed the ship's sensor array.

All of the Griffins sensors were tied into the aircrew's helmets and digital readouts and could be seen either on the helmet visor or on a HUD, heads-up display, in the cockpit. Digital data link capability allowed both the computer and sensor data to be sent between the Griffin and the Dragon Flight ground stations.

In Greek mythology, a Griffin was a winged, eagle-headed lion, and that was a good description for this far-seeing, hard-hitting machine. But, even though the chopper cops were always in the news, it was usually only the criminals who got a close-up look at the Griffins.

With the recent controversy in the media about the TPF busting environmentalist protestors in the Medicine Bow National Forest the last winter, the Tac Force headquarters in Washington, DC, felt the force needed to mend the public relations fences. And, what better place to show off the chopper cop's aerial equipment than at the nation's biggest airshow. Later in the afternoon, Gunner and Mojo would put the Griffin through its paces for the crowd, and a team from Dragon Flight's Tac platoon would put on a tactical parachute jumping and rappelling demonstration.

Jennings slowly shook his head. "He's got to be nuts to fly that antique that way. He's going to tear a wing off that thing if he's not careful."

"Never happen," Mugabe said. "That old bird's built like a fucking tank." Mojo did much of the maintenance work on the Corsair and he knew that even though the fighter was over fifty years old, it was every bit as good as it had been the day it left the Chance Vought factory in 1948. In fact, since certain parts had been replaced with stronger, more reliable modern components, it was probably a far better airplane than it had been back then. And it certainly wasn't showing its age today as it went from one aerobatic maneuver to the next.

In the cockpit of the Corsair, the pilot grinned broadly as he moved the control stick to the right and went into an aileron roll. TPF Lieutenant Rick "Wolfman" Wolff was doing what he liked to do best—flying. And he was flying his favorite fixed wing aircraft. He stopped his roll in an inverted position and, holding a slight forward pressure on the stick, passed over the crowd upside down at over three hundred fifty miles an hour.

Normally, Wolff could be found in the pilot's seat of a

Dragon Flight Griffin chopper. But today, he had changed his dark-blue Tac Force flight suit for a pair of blue jeans, a leather flight helmet, and a battered World War Two leather flying jacket with a "Blood Chit" on the back and the insignia of Marine Fighter Squadron VMF-214, the famous Black Sheep Squadron, on the breast. He looked like an extra in a grade B World War Two fighter pilot movie, and that was exactly how he wanted to look.

Even though his Corsair was a later model than the ones that had faced the deadly Japanese Zeros over the Pacific, Wolff saw himself blazing a path of glory across the Pacific skies. Rolling out of his inverted flight, he glanced down at his instrument panel and saw that he was coming up onto his reserve fuel. It was time to land.

After getting landing clearance from the tower, Wolff lined up with the end of the runway, dropped his flaps, and came in for a carrier-style landing as gracefully as a seagull landing on a sandy beach. He taxied the big fighter to its parking spot and switched off the Pratt and Whitney. When the thunder of the exhaust died away, Wolff pulled off his leather helmet and hit the shoulder harness release. Sliding the canopy back, he stepped out onto the fighter's gull wing with a big grin on his face, looking every inch like a Navy pilot returning to his Pacific fleet carrier after a successful combat mission.

Mugabe walked up to him shaking his head. "Man, you've got to watch those low-level passes," he said. "If you hit a sudden gust of wind down that low, you're going to splash that thing all over the concrete."

Wolff ran his hand through his long blond hair. "You're sounding more and more like Red each day," he grinned. "When the day comes that I screw up a simple low-level pass, they can pull my license."

"When that day comes," Mojo replied, "they're going to have to scrape your ass out of the wreckage first to get to your wallet to pull your license."

"Mojo, my man." Wolff sounded offended. "You know you're not supposed to talk about crashing. It's bad luck. You have to be real careful what you say around a hot-shot, air-show pilot like me. You might shake my confidence and cause me to make a mistake."

The black gunner slowly looked Wolff up and down. "Yo Momma."

Rick Wolff and Jumal Mugabe had been flying together since the earliest days of the Tac Force Dragon Flight. They had both been in the first Griffin helicopter conversion class and first teamed up at the start of the weapons training phase. At first, Wolff hadn't known what to make of the muscular black with the single gold earring, the bushy mustache, the shaved head and a jive-ass attitude. But, after the first day on the gunnery range he knew that he was working with a master of aerial gunners a real left-hand seat ace.

That night the two men discovered that they had a lot in common besides their love of flying choppers. Wolff had not been able to fly in any of the recent wars throughout the world, so he was enthralled by Mugabe's combat stories. The burly black gunner had flown for several of the government's secret armies as well as for the CIA and DEA. He had finally gotten that out of his system when he had stopped a bullet in the jungle and had tried civilian life for a while. Finding that boring, he immediately signed up for the Tac Police when they had started recruiting.

When the Griffin school ended, Wolff graduated at the top of the class and he requested that Mugabe be assigned as the gunner on his chopper. Since then, the two men had worked together and played together both on and off duty.

"When are you and Gunner going to do your thing in the Griffin?" Wolff asked.

Mojo checked his watch. "We're on in half an hour if

they keep to the schedule."

"I'd better refuel now so I don't miss it."

The Brinks armored car maintained a steady fifty-five miles an hour along US highway 80 heading west from Reno to Sacramento on the way to San Francisco.

Even in the age of universal electronic transfer of monies, there was still a need for hard cash money, particularly in a place like Reno. Even though all the slot machines, blackjack, and craps tables in the casinos would accept a player's personal Unicard as well as it would chips or cash on the table, most gamblers wanted to feel the green when they won. But, since the big winners were always the casinos, there was always a great deal of currency that had to be moved to the banks. Once a week, the armored car made a run from Reno to the Federal Reserve Bank in San Francisco with millions of dollars in the back.

The driver and shotgun rider on this run were old hands at the armored car business. They had been making the long five hour trip for years and, while it sounded like an exciting job, it was actually boring as hell. No one in their right mind would even try to knock over a modern armored car.

For one thing, the vehicle was almost impossible to stop with anything short of antitank weapons. Everything on the car was armored to withstand fifty-caliber fire—the tires, the engine, and the cab. Also, the cab was a self-contained unit equipped with an oxygen-over-pressure system to prevent gas attacks on the crew. Once they were locked inside, the crew was immune from gunfire, couldn't be driven out with gas, and were in constant contact with the federal, state, and local police units along their route through an all-frequency radio system.

And, even if the vehicle could be stopped somehow, there was no way that anyone was going to get at the money inside it. The only way to get into the time-lock vault in the back was to use explosives—a lot of explosives, and that would leave little for the criminals to take except shredded paper. Transporting money in a Brinks armored car was as safe as leaving it in a bank. The driver and shotgun rider were talking about their favorite subject, women drivers, and were placing their bets on how many beaver shots they'd catch in the next hundred miles. They were on the stretch of flat desert west of Reno, and the steady stream of traffic heading for the casinos should provide plenty of good viewing opportunities.

Suddenly, a dark shadow flashed over the top of their truck and stopped, blocking out the bright spring desert sun.

"What the hell is that?" The shotgun rider leaned forward and craned his neck to look up through the bulletproof Lexan windshield. Keeping pace a few feet above and off to the right side of the armored car was a desert-camouflaged helicopter gunship. The turret in the nose of the ship slowly turned to zero in on the cab.

The shotgunner didn't waste a second. He reached out and grabbed the radio mike from the clip on the dashboard. "May Day! May Day! Any station! This is the Brinks armored car six niner heading west on US 80 at milepost forty-six. We are under attack by an armed helicopter. May Day! May Day!"

CHAPTER 2

The Reno Airshow

As soon as the last of the Navy War Birds had finished their aerobatic routines, it was time for Gunner and Mugabe to show the crowd what a Tac Force Griffin could do.

"Showtime," Gunner announced as he opened the right-hand cockpit door of the Griffin and slid into the pilot's seat.

"Let's do it," Mugabe answered. The co-pilot turned and whistled at the six Tac cops dressed all in black, police tactical uniforms standing by the tail of the ship. When their leader looked his way, Mojo pumped his arm up and down in the classic move-out signal. The six men grabbed they gear and scrambled into the rear of the Griffin, sliding the door shut behind them.

As Mojo climbed into the left-hand side of the ship and buckled his shoulder harness, Gunner triggered the switch to his throat mike. "Reno Tower," he radioed. "This is Dragon One Four. Request permission to crank up and taxi."

"Reno Tower, permission granted. Clear to taxi to runway two."

As soon as he heard the tower give the clearance over his helmet earphones, Mugabe began reading the turbine start-up checklist. As Gunner's gloved fingers flew over the Griffin's switches and controls, he called out the completion of each item to his co-pilot.

"Battery, on. Internal power. on. Inverter switch, off. RPM warning light, on. Fuel, both main and start, on. RPM governor, decrease."

Mugabe looked to the rear to check that both sides of the ship were clear and saw that the ground crew had moved the spectators safely away from the main rotors path. "Main rotor, clear. Crank her up!"

Reaching down with his right hand, Gunner twisted the throttle on the collective control stick open to the Flight Idle position and pulled the starting trigger. In the rear of the ship, the portside GE turbine burst to life with a screeching whine and the hot smell of burning JP-4. Over their heads, the four-bladed main rotor slowly began to turn, moving faster and faster as the turbine spooled up. As soon as the portside turbine was running at 40 percent RPM, the pilot switched over to the starboard and fired it up.

As the turbine RPM's built and the main rotor came up to full speed, the pilot held the throttle at flight idle and watched the needles on the exhaust gas temperature and RPM gauges come up. Everything was in the green.

He twisted the throttle all the way up against the stop. The whine built to a bone-shaking scream as the turbines ran up all the way to 6,000 RPM. Overhead, the main rotor was a blur. Everything was still in the green.

He flipped the RPM governor switch to increase and the turbines screamed even higher at 6,700 RPM's. The instruments were still green.

Gunner backed his throttle down to flight idle as he keyed his throat mike. "Tower, this is Dragon One Four, beginning taxi now."

"Tower, roger."

Cocking the throttle open as he gently hauled up on the collective, Gunner lifted the Griffin off the tarmac in a low, ground-effect hover. He nudged down on the rudder pedal, swinging the ship's tail around to line up with the taxiway. As he taxied past the crowd, the pilot was grinning under his face shield. He was very much aware of the effect the Griffin had on first sight. Few civilians had ever seen a Dragon Flight chopper up close and it was a shock.

Most people were used to seeing police forces flying civilian-type helicopters, not bad-ass gunships. Except for their markings, most police choppers looked relatively tame. But everything about the Griffin screamed "Don't mess with me." From the bug-eyed, nose sensor array and chin turret weapon to the sleek, swept-back tail fins, the dark-blue Griffin looked positively lethal. And it was just as lethal as it looked—any criminal who had ever come up against one could vouch for that. Gunner couldn't demonstrate his ship's lethality today, but he could sure as hell show them what she could do in the air.

Once he was lined up at the end of the runway, Gunner held the ship in a low hover as he keyed his mike. "Tower, this Dragon One Four. Ready to take off."

"Roger, One Four, you're clear."

Twisting the throttle all the way up against the stop, the pilot pushed forward on the cyclic control stick. The chopper's tail came up as she started down the runway in a classic gunship takeoff, her skids bare inches off the concrete runway.

As soon as his air speed came up, Gunner hauled up on the collective, pulling max pitch on the rotor blades. The sleek, dark-blue machine rocketed up into the air. The bright desert sun flashed on the yellow letters U.S.T.P.F. painted on the Griffin's belly and the number "One Four" on the underside of her nose as Gunner banked away to gain altitude.

High over the airfield, the sleek, dark-blue Griffin flashed through the sky as Gunner put his ship through her aerobatic paces for the crowd. There was more to Gunner's performance today than just giving the public a chance to see what the TPF gunship could do in the air. Gunner wasn't a hotshot airshow pilot like Wolff, but as far as he was concerned, he was every bit as good a chopper driver as the flashy Dragon Flight leader and he was going to prove it.

In the rear compartment of the Griffin, a six-man parachute team from Dragon Flight's tactical platoon waited for their cue. The twenty-two-man Tac platoon was Dragon Flight's ground muscle, a development of the old police SWAT team concept. But, where traditional SWAT teams were limited in their capabilities, the Tac platoon was as highly trained and as well-equipped as an Army Ranger unit. In fact, they received much of their training from the Rangers, and today they were going to put on a parachute demonstration that no other police unit in the nation could pull off.

In the seat closest to the right-hand door, TPF Lieutenant Jack "Zoomie" Zumwald grinned broadly under his face shield as Gunner sent the Griffin into an inside loop. Gunner didn't have as smooth a hand on the controls as Wolff did, but he could still drive a Griffin. As the ship reached the top of the loop and went into an Immelmann turn, Zoomie made one last check of his jump gear and tapped his jump partner on the shoulder. The Tac cop gave him a thumbs-up as Zoomie unbuckled his seat belt and slid the side door back.

The parachute demonstration today was going to be complicated, but it was sure to be a crowd pleaser. The six Tac cops were going to exit the chopper in pairs at different altitudes. Zoomie and his partner would free fall in a halo jump, the next pair would make a normal low-altitude jump, and the last pair would make a fast rappel. If they had the timing right, all three teams would hit the ground at the same time, their weapons blazing with blank ammunition.

Zoomie keyed his throat mike and called up to Mojo, who

was coordinating the jump. "First team's go back here."

"Copy," Mojo called back. "We're coming up on five thousand feet. Wait for the count."

Zoomie and his partner took their jump positions in the open door and leaned out over the airport far below as the rotor blast buffeted their jump suits.

"Get ready," Mojo radioed back to them. "Mark! Five, four, three, two, one. Jump!"

Their arms held tightly at their sides, both men dove headfirst from the chopper. As soon as Zoomie and his partner were clear, Gunner put the Griffin into a steep dive. The second low-altitude team would jump at a thousand feet and he had to get there before the free-fall team did.

Zoomie assumed the spread-eagle, free-fall position and watched the Griffin keeping pace with him as it dove for the ground. When it looked like the Griffin was getting away from him, he tucked his arms in tightly to his side again to increase the speed of his fall. He had to be right behind the chopper when the second team exited the ship so they could open their parachutes together at the same time.

A few seconds later, when Gunner pulled the Griffin out of her dive, Zoomie and his partner were right behind him. Suddenly, two more Tac cops exited the ship, free-falling for an instant before they popped their chutes. Zoomie and his partner pulled their D rings right above them and the four parachutes opened almost as one.

"They're gone," Mojo said, looking over his shoulder through the open side door. Gunner put the ship into a steep dive again to reach the five-hundred-foot level where the last team would rappel to the ground. So far, the demonstration had gone off like clockwork. In the back of the ship, the last team quickly rigged their rappelling ropes to the tie-downs on the floor plates. After hooking the ropes to their rappelling harnesses, they took their positions standing backward in the open doors.

Mugabe also had his eyes on the altimeter and, as it approached the five hundred-foot mark, he called back, "Ready!"

Gunner leveled out and brought the chopper to a complete halt in the air. "Go!" Mugabe radioed.

Dropping their soiled ropes to the ground, the two Tac cops stepped out of the hovering chopper for a fast rappel to the runway below. The four parachuting cops caught up with the rappellers halfway to the ground and steered their chutes in close to them so they would all land together as a team.

The Tac cops on the rappelling ropes had just reached the ground when the emergency call from the armored car came in over the chopper's all frequency radio scanner. "May Day! May Day! Any station! This is the Brinks armored car six niner heading west on US 80 at milepost forty-six. We are under attack…"

Wolff was sitting on the wing of his Corsair waiting for Gunner's demonstration to end so he could join up with the other war birds for a last mass flyover to mark the end of the day's activities. Out of habit, he had tuned his radio to the Griffin's tactical frequency and was monitoring the radio chatter as Gunner dropped off his passengers.

When he heard the call from the armored car, he scrambled for the cockpit, pulling on his flight helmet as he dropped into the seat. His finger stabbed for the starter before he even had his shoulder harness buckled. In seconds the big Pratt and Whitney radial engine was bellowing as the prop blades started spinning.

"Tower, this is Corsair Foxtrot Four Uniform," Wolff radioed as he waved the spectators away from the nose of his ship. "I have a police emergency," he radioed. "Clear the runway for an emergency takeoff." Wolff didn't even give the tower a chance to answer but started taxiing immediately for the end of the runway.

"Foxtrot Four Uniform," the tower radioed in a panic. "Hold your position, you are not—"

"This is Four Uniform," Wolff snapped back. "This is a police emergency and I'm taking off. Clear that damned runway! Now!"

To keep from having to listen to more nonsense from the tower, he switched his radio over to the TPF tactical channel and keyed his throat mike. "Dragon One Four," he called to Gunner. "This is the Wolfman, I'll be taking off in two zero. What's your heading?"

"This is One Four X-Ray," Mugabe answered. "We're at two thousand on a bearing of one-niner-seven."

"Good copy, I'll be there ASAP."

As soon as he was lined up with the end of the runway, Wolff looked around and saw that the tower had gotten their fingers out of their asses and had cleared the traffic away. He shoved the Corsair's throttle all the way forward into full military power. The big four-bladed prop clawed the air as the 2,300 horsepower radial engine howled at full power. The Corsair shot forward as if it had been fired from a cannon.

He pulled the tail up as soon as he had elevator control and, when the air-speed indicator passed a hundred miles an hour, he lifted the ship off the tarmac. No sooner had his wheels left the ground than Wolff hit the gear retraction lever, sucking the wheels up to clean the airframe. He was doing over two hundred miles an hour before he was even a hundred feet off the ground. As soon as he had cleared the airfield, he banked the Corsair up onto one wingtip and sped after the Griffin at 450 miles an hour.

The top speed of the Griffin was only 275 miles an hour, so the powerful Navy fighter caught up with the chopper only a few miles away from the airfield. Wolff keyed his mike as he throttled back to keep pace with the slower helicopter. "Dragon

One Four, this is the Wolfman, I'm right on your tail. Have you heard any more from the armored car?"

"One Four," Gunner replied. "That's a negative. I can't raise him on the radio."

"Have you called this in to Denver?"

"That's affirm," Gunner radioed back. "I also alerted the Nevada State Patrol and they're sending a ground unit to that location."

"Roger," Wolff radioed back, falling into the military radio language the war bird pilots used on the airshow circuit. "Keep me informed. Out."

Wolff wasn't too sure what he and Gunner were going to be able to do when they did get to the scene of the hijacking. Neither one of them was armed. Fuck it, he'd worry about that when he got there.

CHAPTER 3

US 80, forty-six miles west of Reno

Since Wolff's Corsair dated from the era before air-to-air radar, he was completely blind to what they were flying into. Therefore, he flew high top cover while Mojo activated the Griffin's radar and targeting sensors to search for the armed helicopters that the armored car crew had reported.

"I'm not picking up anything on the bandits," he told Gunner. "Just a few cars on the road. They must be hiding behind a hill."

The pilot keyed his mike as he pulled back on his cyclic control to gain altitude. "Wolfman, we're not getting anything on the sensors down here. I'm going up a little higher in case they're in defilade."

"Roger."

In the left-hand seat, Mugabe's fingers flew over his sensor controls, tuning them to maximum sensitivity, but even up higher, he still couldn't pick up the choppers. Usually he could spot a bird at twenty miles and tell you if it was a male or a female, but he wasn't getting diddly today. Maybe they were too late and the chopper bandits had fled the scene of the crime. Finally he located a truck-size mass of metal sitting stationary along the side of the highway, but there was no indication of a helicopter anywhere in the vicinity. "We're coming up on the truck," Mugabe announced as he looked up through the canopy. "There it is!" he pointed.

The Brinks armored car was sitting off on the side of the road with its rear doors gaping open. As Gunner pushed the nose of his ship down to fly a low pass over it, the men saw that the cab had been blasted open and two bodies lay beside it in the sand. Probably the Brinks guards.

As if from out of thin air, a sinister-looking angular, red-colored helicopter suddenly appeared. From the shape of the forward fuselage and stub wings, Mojo instantly identified it as being an Italian-built Mangusta II gunship, the hottest armed helicopter in Europe. And he saw what looked to be antitank missiles hanging from the ship's underwing pylons.

What in the hell was an armed Mangusta doing in the United States?

Gunner switched over to the international emergency channel and keyed his mike. "Unknown aircraft, this is the Tactical Police Force. Land your aircraft immediately and step out onto the ground. How copy? Over."

Instead of answering, the Mangusta broke away to the left, and the two flyers saw that a second Mangusta had been flying right behind the first. Gunner banked away to follow the first ship.

"Unknown aircraft, this is the Tactical Pol—"

"We have lock on!" Mugabe shouted, his fingers stabbing the controls of his countermeasures panel for the decoy flares and the ECM radar jammer. "Get us outta here! Fast!"

From two thousand one hundred feet above the armored car, Wolff saw the second Mangusta turn in the air to start its gun run on the helpless Griffin. "Gunner?" he shouted over the radio. "Break right!"

Sparkles of flame blossomed from the nose of the Mangusta as it opened up on Gunner's Griffin. As Gunner desperately tried to get his ship out of the line of fire, Mojo clenched his hands in helpless rage. With no ammunition for his turret weapons, they were sitting ducks.

Just then, a flash of dark navy-blue dove down on top of the Mangusta. For an instant, Mojo thought that the Corsair was going to collide with the chopper, but at the last moment, Wolff banked away, his belly bare inches away from the chopper's canopy. The hurricane-force winds from his prop wash made the Mangusta stagger in the air and lose lift.

Wolff pulled out of his dive and zoomed back up as Gunner hit the turbine over-rev switch and pushed the nose of his ship down to get every last mile an hour he could get out of it. Their only chance was to try to outrun it.

When Wolff saw the telltale thin black smoke pour out of the Griffin's turbines, he knew that Gunner had turned the wick up all the way and was going to try to make a run for it. He also knew that it probably wasn't going to work. Gunner's unarmed ship was no match for the Mangusta. If he remembered what he had read, the Italian chopper was quite a bit faster and just as maneuverable as the Griffin. A dogfight or a drag race between the two helicopters could only have one result—dead chopper cops.

Even though his Corsair wasn't armed, either, Wolff thought that he might be able to use his fighter's greater speed to keep the Mangusta busy while Gunner and Mojo made good their escape.

"Run for it!" he shouted over the radio. "I'll keep him busy."

As he maneuvered his fighter into position to make another run on the Mangusta, Wolff also knew that he was putting himself at risk of getting shot down, too. Highly maneuverable armed helicopters had downed jet fighters in several wars starting with that gunship jockey from the Air Cav who had aced a Cambodian MiG-17 with an AH-I Cobra during

Vietnam. Since then, it had been done several more times, particularly by Israeli pilots. In aerial combat, maneuverability was everything and could make up for slower airspeed. He'd have to watch his ass carefully or he'd find his name on the list of the dumb-shit fighter pilots in fast planes who had figured a slow-moving helicopter to be easy meat.

But his gambit had worked. The Mangusta turned to deal with him. Now, he had to figure out what to do next.

Wolff saw the reflection of the sun off the chopper's spinning rotor blades change as the pilot pulled coarse pitch to the blades. Only another chopper pilot would have caught that and known that he was being set up for a gun run.

Suddenly, the Mangusta snapped her tail around and was lined up on him, her nose turret seeking him out. But Wolff was ready for it.

He chopped his throttle, slammed his control stick over on the far right-hand corner, and dumped his flaps all at the same time. With the sudden increase in drag and the loss of power, the big fighter came up vertically on one wingtip and almost did a pivot turn.

Had Wolff been flying anything other than a Corsair, he would have stalled out and fallen from the sky. As it was, the Navy fighter's big gull wings gave him just enough lift to maintain control as the stream of tracer fire flashed through the empty sky over his head.

Switching over to coarse pitch on his prop controls, he firewalled the throttle. The Pratt and Whitney bellowed as the four-bladed prop clawed the air and pulled him around in a tight turn toward the Mangusta. Sucking up his flaps to clean his wings and gain airspeed, he dove on the gunship again.

As the Mangusta filled his gunsight, his finger instinctively squeezed the gun trigger on his control stick. But, the four 20mm cannons mounted in the fighters wings were there only for looks—they were incapable of firing.

Even though no fire came from the Corsair's wings, the Mangusta's pilot threw his ship out of the way. As he evaded, the gunner swung the chopper's nose turret around to track him and squeezed off a quick burst at the diving Corsair.

Wolff was not able to get out of the line of fire in time. He hauled back on his control stick to pull out of his dive when several 20mm rounds caught him. Explosions rocked the Corsair. A bright flash of flame from the nose of the plane seared Wolff's vision and the starboard exhaust started belching orange-red flame and thick black smoke.

His eyes flicked down to the instrument panel. The needle of the cylinder-head temperature gauge had shot up into the red zone. One of those rounds had hit his engine, and if he didn't shut it down quickly, it could catch on fee. Wolff racked his fighter around in the other direction and headed for the highway. There was little traffic on the road and it would make a good runway.

The Mangusta didn't follow as Wolff headed for a landing on the highway below. As soon as Wolff put his landing gear down and lined up on his approach, the chopper gunship dropped down to sagebrush level and quickly disappeared to the east.

Gunner had watched the dogfight, and when he saw Wolff break away from the fight, he brought his Griffin back. He flared out for a landing next to the Corsair right as Wolff stepped out of the cockpit with a small foam fire extinguisher in his hands. The Corsairs engine was still smoking, but there were no flames. Wolff sprayed the foam on the engine through the front of the cowling just to make sure.

"You okay?" Mugabe shouted over to him as he reached back for the Griffin's fire extinguisher.

"Yeah!" Wolff shouted back. "Bring that thing over here!

Quick!"

Mojo sprinted over with the big fire extinguisher in his arms and sprayed more foam in the rear of the cowling on the hot exhaust manifold. Steam rose from the hot engine, but the smoke died away.

As soon as Wolff was satisfied that the Corsair wasn't going to burn to a puddle of melted aluminum and ashes, the two cops walked over to check out the armored car. Both of the Brinks guards were dead, shot at close range. The back of the armored car was completely empty. Whatever it had been carrying was gone now.

Gunner immediately went back to the Griffin to report the situation to the Nevada State Patrol and request an ambulance for the dead guards.

While Gunner was on the radio, Mugabe inspected the 20mm holes in the Corsair. Along with the engine damage, one aileron had been shot halfway off and there were two holes in the fuselage right behind the cockpit. "Right off hand, my man," he told Wolff, "I'd say that you bit off a little more than you could chew this time."

The pilot ran his hand through his hair and stared to the east. "I'm going to get that motherfucker," he growled. "I owe him for this."

"I'd sure as hell make sure that I had some ammunition on board before I tried anything like that again," Mojo cautioned. "Whoever those fuckers are, they're playing for keeps."

"I'll have ammo the next time," Wolff said grimly. "You can bet your sweet ass on that."

"I've got the State Patrol on their way," Gunner announced as he walked up to them. "And they're bringing the meat wagon."

There was little for the Nevada Patrol to do at the robbery site other than bag the bodies and take a report from the chopper cops. The crime lab people would go over the armored car one inch at a time later, but Wolff didn't think that they'd find anything they would use other than the ballistics information from the wounds in the guards' bodies. This had been too professional for any obvious clues like fingerprints to have been left behind.

As soon as the police wrecker came for the armored car, the desert was clean again, as if the attack had never occurred. Except, of course, for the downed Corsair.

"You ready to go?" Mojo asked.

"I'm not going back with you." Wolff shook his head. "I'm staying here with the plane. Just get the recovery people on their way ASAP, so I don't have to spend the night here."

"You sure?"

"Yeah," Wolff nodded. "I'm sure. I don't want to leave her alone."

Mugabe smiled; he knew how Wolff felt.

Wolff knew that it would be several hours before Mugabe could get a recovery team out from Reno to retrieve the downed Corsair. So, while he waited, he busied himself by folding the wings manually and attaching the towing hooks to the main landing gear. When the truck did arrive, it would be a simple task to winch the fighter onto the back of the flatbed and tie it down for the road trip back to the airport. Making the ship airworthy again, however, would be another matter.

Not only had the engine been damaged, there were several large 20mm holes in the airframe as well. The battle damage would have to be repaired and the entire plane inspected before it could take to the air again.

Wolff sat on the leading edge of the wing and gazed out over the desert. Whoever those people in the Mangustas had been, he was going to see that they paid for this. Not only had they tried to kill him, but worse than that, they had shot up his

Corsair. Wolff was used to having people trying to kill him—that went along with wearing the TPF uniform. But nobody messed around with his war bird. He vowed that he'd have someone's ass in a sling for this.

CHAPTER 4

Western Region TPF Headquarters, Denver

The Dragon Flight home base was buzzing as the chopper cops waited for the return of Dragon One Four and the men who had been at the Reno airshow. Everyone had heard about the dramatic aerial armored car robbery and Wolff having been shot down by the chopper bandits. In his office on the ground floor, TPF Captain J.D. "Buzz" Corcran went over the report of the action one more time as he waited.

The Dragon Flight Commander was a barrel-chested man of fifty-five who looked at least ten years younger than his actual age. He wore his hair cut military short to hide the fact that it was rapidly thinning and did sit-ups every night to try to stave off the slight paunch that threatened to get out of control. He wore his dark-blue TPF uniform proudly, and the brightly polished, silver wings of an Army helicopter pilot were pinned on his uniform blouse right above the gold TPF police pilot wings.

Thirty-four years ago, Buzz had been a twenty-one-year-old, hot rock, Huey gunship pilot with the 1st Air Cavalry Division in Vietnam. He had picked up his nickname when he had made a high-speed, low-level run over the division headquarters at An Khe after a very successful mission. Unfortunately, he had made his run right over the general's personal latrine and the general had been on his throne when the rotor blast from the low-flying Huey had tipped it over. Corcran had been lucky not to have been sent to pick up cigarette butts along the Ho Chi Minh trail for the rest of his tour.

When he got out of the hospital at the end of his second tour with the Air Cav, and his fourth wound, he decided that he needed to find a less exciting occupation—at least one that didn't involve him getting shot at on a daily basis. He resigned his commission from the Army and went into the helicopter maintenance business in California. After a year of that, though, he was bored out of his mind and answered an ad looking for chopper pilots for the California State Highway Patrol. It turned out that cruising up and down the crowded freeways looking for speeders wasn't exciting enough for him either and he soon joined up as a pilot with the Federal Drug Enforcement Agency.

That had been much more fun, particularly when President Bush's war on drugs had heated up. He had led the first contingent of DEA gunships into Colombia and Peru to do battle with the cocaine barons and their private armies. When the Tactical Police Force had been formed in 1996, he transferred over from the DEA and had been chosen to command the first Dragon Flight.

Buzz enjoyed running Dragon Flight, but he resented being stuck behind a desk most of the time. And, as the polished, proudly worn wings on his uniform proclaimed, he was still a chopper pilot at heart. Each year he managed to sneak away from the endless piles of paperwork and spend enough time behind the controls of one of the Griffin gunships to keep his TPF flight status active so he could continue to wear his cherished wings.

Under his command, the Western Region Dragon Flight had been developed into the hardest-hitting unit of the entire TPF. But keeping their reputation intact was not an easy job, particularly at times like this. The fiasco with the armored car robbery had brought his unit a great deal of criticism from the other federal law-enforcement agencies. But this was not the first time that the TPF had been criticized and it sure as hell wouldn't be the last.

The TPF was the youngest of the federal services and the older federal law enforcement agencies resented the Tac Force muscling in on what they considered to be their home turf. Buzz really didn't care what the other agencies thought about his Dragon Flight. He knew that the Tac Force had been created specifically to keep that kind of interagency backbiting from interfering with the war on crime.

By the mid-1990's, it had become all too apparent that the United States was losing the war against crime. Faced with a rapidly growing situation that was not responding to the more traditional methods, Congress finally realized that the formation of a national police force was an absolute necessity. The existing federal law enforcement organizations—the FBI, the Federal Marshals, the DEA, the Sky Marshals, the Customs Police and the Immigration Service—could not contain the growing crime problem.

One of the main reasons they couldn't was that, all too often, their efforts were scattered and uncoordinated. What was needed was one uniform federal organization that would combine the law-enforcement functions of all the old organizations under one command. One of President Bush's last official acts at the end of his second term in office was to form a national police organization, the United States Tactical Police Force.

The mission of the new Tac Force was to stand between the criminal element in the nation and the citizenry. They were given the authority to preserve the peace and uphold the law anywhere in the fifty-one United States and could override local authority. If a crime was being committed anywhere in the country, the TPFs job was to stop it.

There had been a great deal of resistance to the TPF at

first, particularly from the professional liberals and entrenched corrupt public officials. But the old methods had been proven worthless and the very fabric of American life was being shredded by the new barbarians. The time had come to give the country back to its citizens.

The first line weapon of the TPF in this war against crime were the Dragon Flights, the Tac Police in the sky. The chopper cops who flew the Griffins were a new breed of police officer, the elite of the elite troops of law enforcement. With the cutback in American military forces in the late nineties, men who would have been hot rock fighter jocks in an earlier era were now flying Griffins for the TPF instead.

These were the new "Top Guns"—young, quick, and fearless, and they saw themselves as the nation's first line of defense against violent crime. They were willing to die to protect those whom they had sworn to defend, but only after taking a few of the enemy with them.

Many of the chopper cop's leaders were military veterans who had learned their trade in Vietnam, Nicaragua, and the Middle East. They viewed the battle against crime as a war, and used their combat experience to good advantage against gangs who were all too often armed and equipped as well as many armies. Usually the Tac Force enjoyed air superiority with the Dragon Flights, but this armored car incident proved that even Dragon Flight was vulnerable.

Buzz reached out and hit the intercom button on his desk. "Ruby, what's the latest ETA on Wolff and Gunner?"

"They're landing now, sir."

"Get 'em in here ASAP!" Buzz growled.

"Yes, sir."

The two chopper cops were ushered right on into Buzz's office and found the Dragon Flight commander sitting behind his desk.

"I've got the report on your armored car robbery," Buzz said before either one of them could even say hello. His fingers tapped a thick folder on his desk. "Your aerial bandits got away with over five million in cash."

Wolff whistled softly. "That's a lot of robbery."

"It sure as hell is," Buzz snapped. "And if you guys hadn't lost them, I'd be putting this in the dead file instead of having to answer Washington's questions about how they got away from you."

"Captain," Gunner said. "We were unarmed and were lucky that we didn't get shot down. Whoever those guys were, they weren't playing around."

"I've got 20mm holes in my Corsair to prove it, sir," Wolff added.

"Speaking of your private aircraft," Buzz snapped back. "Washington also wants to know what in the hell a private plane was doing taking part in a TPF operation."

Wolff started to answer, but Buzz put up his hand. "Also, I had a call from the FAA at the Reno airport wanting to know why you violated several safety regulations when you made an unauthorized takeoff."

"But it was an emergency..." Wolff started to protest. "I needed to—"

"I don't fucking want to hear it," Buzz interrupted him. "You people were sent down there to make a good impression on the public and you made assholes out of yourselves."

"If we'd had ammunition on board, sir..." Gunner tried to defend himself.

"But you didn't," Buzz snapped back. "And you went charging into a live fire situation with nothing more than your dicks in your hands and got shot down. Do you know how this makes us look?"

Neither one of the pilots said anything.

"The next time I see you two hotshots, I want to see your full reports on this incident in your hands. Dismissed!"

Wolff and Gunner left without a word.

On the way out of Buzz's office, Wolff stopped off at the communications section to talk to the woman sitting behind the radio console. "I see that you still have your ass intact," she said, looking the pilot up and down. "The last guy to go in there this morning was carried out on a stretcher with an IV bottle plugged into his arm."

"I must admit that he's in fine form today," Wolff grinned. "What's biting him?"

She raised one eyebrow. "Other than that dumb fucking stunt you and Gunner pulled in Reno?"

TPF Sergeant Ruby Jenkins was the brains and voice of Dragon Control, the communications and dispatch center for the Griffins of Dragon Flight. A small, trim, redheaded woman in her early fifties, if anyone other than Buzz knew what was going on, she would.

Wolff had the good graces to look somewhat embarrassed. "Other than that, I mean."

"Well..." she started out. "Washington's been on the horn to him all morning. The regional commander is deep in his shit about fuel expenditures. And, of course, there is the small matter of two of his pilots letting a Brinks armored car get robbed right under their noses."

"Other than that," she said, "I'd say that it's pretty much a normal day around here. You should stop in here more often so you'll have a better idea of what we have to put up with on a daily basis."

Although she usually employed the vocabulary of a Marine Drill instructor—and the volume—Ruby was very protective of the Dragon Flight officers she worked with, and particularly of their commander. Because of that, she was known to the chopper cops as Mom. Mom always had a ready shoulder to cry on, but she also had a quick boot in the ass for anyone who screwed up "her" Tactical Police Force. And, as far as she was concerned, Rick Wolff was messing with her force today.

Mom was a legend in federal law enforcement circles and could get away with about anything that she wanted to do in the TPF. After doing a short enlistment in the Army right out of high school, she had become one of the first female special agents in the F.B.I., where she had made a name for herself with her handling of dangerous undercover assignments against terrorist and drug operations.

Her reputation for tackling difficult assignments had been crowned when she had tracked down the assassins who had poisoned California's governor and his antiwar activist wife at the dedication of the Peace Activist Memorial in San Francisco's McArthur Park in 1992. The deaths had been caused by strychnine and angel dust-laden cocaine that had been offered in the "hospitality room" provided by the event's organizers. At first the poisonings had appeared to be accidental, just another incident of bad drugs. But Ruby had picked up a rumor on the street that the poisoned cocaine had been planted there by expatriate South African mercenaries working for a radical conservative group.

Ruby had doggedly followed the rumor, tracking the Afrikaners to their operating base in Northern Ireland, but the Irish authorities had refused to extradite them. The South Africans were a valuable part of Northern Ireland's foreign policy arm and they were not about to compromise that over the death of one of their loudest critics.

The unwelcome international publicity that had resulted from that episode, however, had worked against her. While on her next assignment, her cover was blown and she had almost been killed. Reassigned to a boring desk job while she recovered from her wounds, Ruby had jumped at the chance to become the communications officer for Dragon Flight when the job was offered to her.

She was still stuck behind a desk, but at least she wasn't stuck shuffling papers anymore. Now she was in the electronic center of everything that Dragon Flight did. Ruby Jenkins might be affectionately known as Mom, but she ruled her electronic kingdom with an iron hand. And, as far as she was concerned, a big part of her job was keeping the pilots in line.

"There's a briefing scheduled for sixteen hundred and I'd strongly advise you to get your shit together before he talks to you again"

"What's up," Wolff asked intently.

"Come to the briefing and find out."

CHAPTER 5

The TPF Flight Line, Denver

On his way to the pilot's ready room to write his report, Wolff stopped off at the Griffin flight line to check on his ship, Dragon One Zero. When he had left for the airshow, it had been taken off line for maintenance and he wanted to see if it was flight-ready yet. The flight line was bustling with activity as Wolff made his way over to his chopper. Several of the inspection and maintenance panels were propped open, but he didn't see anyone working on the machine and he couldn't tell what was being done to it.

Wolff looked around and spotted a big, burly man waving a clipboard in the air as he yelled something at a cowering man dressed in mechanics' overalls.

"Yo, Red!" he called out. The man didn't respond, so the pilot walked over to him and, as he got closer, he could hear the tail end of a royal ass-chewing.

"...and I swear to Christ," the big man yelled in the mechanic's face, "if I ever see you ever do anything like that again, I'm going to shove that tool box all the way up your ass until it's stuck in your throat."

The big man took a breath. "And then, I'm going to, to..." He paused, unable to think of new, even more horrifying threats than the ones he had already used. "Oh, fuck it!" he roared. "Just get the hell out of my sight."

The mechanic scrambled to disappear as fast as he could when the big man, Eric "Red" Larsen, the Dragon Flight maintenance officer and the crew chief for Dragon One Zero, turned to face the pilot. "What the fuck do you want?" he snarled around the end of the dead cigar butt clamped between his teeth.

"Red!" Wolff grinned. "Is that any way to talk to your favorite pilot."

Red spat a fragment of well-chewed tobacco onto the tarmac and shifted the cigar butt to the other side of his mouth. "I haven't time for this shit today, Wolfman. I'm busy. So, what the fuck do you want?"

"Since you put it that way," the pilot said, "I just wanted to find out what you're doing to One Zero. The panels are open and no one's working on her. Buzz has got a wild hair up his ass and I just want to make sure that your boys are on the ball so my Griffin will be ready when he decides to send me to Bumfuck, Ethiopia, for extended camel patrol duty. You know I can't afford to have my ride deadlined when the boss says I've got to go."

Red's face went pale. Wolff was hinting that his people were fucking off and no one was allowed to say that about his people except him. He took his work seriously and so did each and every last man and woman who worked for him. If they didn't, they didn't work for him very long. If there was anything in the world that Red gave a shit about, it was helicopters. Red's love affair with rotary-winged flying machines had begun back when he had been a young chopper mechanic in Vietnam. When he had gotten out of the Army, he had started working on police choppers and now, almost thirty years later, he was still in love with helicopters. And he showed that love by seeing that they got the absolute finest mechanical care he and his people could give them.

Normally, Red was a soft-spoken man who looked every one of his fifty odd years, but the remnants of his once-flaming red hair served as a warning of his fiery temper. And the easiest way to reactivate his temper was to say the wrong thing about one of the Griffins. When the police gunship was still on the drawing boards, Red had provided the Bell design team with a great deal of valuable information as to what a real police helicopter ought to be as only a man of his years of experience would know. As a result, he considered the Griffins to be the children he had never had. Woe be it unto any young hotshot pilot or mechanic who abused one of his birds. And, accusing him, or one of his people, of not caring for them properly was even worse.

Red's pale-blue eyes narrowed and his nicotine-stained teeth took a harder grip on the dead cigar butt. "Are you saying that I'm not doing my job?"

"Not at all," Wolff smiled innocently. He knew better than to cross Red when he had a hair up his ass about something. This was just not his day—first Buzz getting on his case about Reno, then Mom biting his ass, and now it looked like Red was definitely on the rag, too. What in the hell was going on around here? The whole place had fallen apart during his short absence and he'd better lay low until whatever was causing all this blew over.

"I was just asking about the status of my chopper." Wolff was careful to keep his voice neutral.

"It'll be done when we're fucking done with it," the maintenance chief snarled around his cigar butt.

"That's just fine with me," Wolff said, raising his hands as if to ward off another verbal blow. "I was just curious, that's all."

Red grunted something unintelligible.

"Have a nice day," Wolff said as he turned to go.

"Asshole!" Red growled.

Wolff didn't even bother to reply to Red's parting shot as he headed for the ready room. It was bad enough that he had to write a report about the Reno affair, he didn't need to have Red on his case, too. If Buzz had a mission for him and One Zero wasn't ready to fly, he could always tell the captain to talk to Red about it.

At a few minutes before four, Wolff and Mugabe walked into the briefing room and the pilot slid into a chair beside Gunner. "Where's Legs?" he asked when he didn't see Gunner's co-pilot.

"She's got the day off." Gunner looked pissed. "So I've got to cover for her again as usual."

"Did you get your report finished for the bossman?" Wolff asked.

Gunner tapped the folder on his lap and grinned. "As nice a piece of fiction as I've ever written."

Wolff smiled back. "Cover your ass, buddy."

"You got it."

The door slammed open and Buzz stormed into the briefing room with a thick folder in his hand and a scowl on his face. "Okay, people," he said as he walked up to the podium. "Let's hold it down. There's a couple of things we have to go over here."

"First off," he said, laying the folder on the podium. "I'm sure that you've all heard the recent media hysteria about 'edge,' that so-called designer drug that's been showing up in Southern California. Well, it's not all hysteria. For once the media morons got something halfway right."

His eyes swept the briefing room. "That stuffs bad news, real bad news, and the government is launching a major interdiction effort to get it stopped before it gets out of control. 'Edge' has the potential to be even worse than the coke epidemic of the eighties and the ice problem of the nineties. It's a highly addictive, sensory stimulator that makes the user feel on top of things without feeling wired like he would on speed or coke. And, since they don't crash when they come down, the users call it 'edge'. They say it gives them an edge on things.

"So far, though, the drug's only shown up in Southern California and the Sunbelt states. But the DEA wants to get it stopped before it spreads any further."

"What's the intelligence on the network that's pushing this stuff?" Simpson asked. "Who are we going up against this time?"

"That's the funny thing about 'edge'," Buzz answered. "They haven't been able to tie it into any of the traditional drug-running operations. The street pushers who've been picked up so far have all been free-lancers, amateurs. And so far, they haven't been able to come up with a distributor. It's almost like a completely new organization has moved in and taken over the streets. And, so far, the drugs seem to be coming up from the South.

"What all this means to us," Buzz continued, "is that we have been ordered to detach two choppers and crews to work with the DEA on a massive drug interdiction operation along the Mexican border."

He scanned the pilots and air crew in the room. "Vargas, Johnson?"

"Yo," Vargas answered.

"You're the team leader in Dragon One Two."

Vargas smiled.

"Browning," Buzz continued. "You and Simpson will accompany him in One Three."

"Yes, sir," Simpson answered.

"Shit," Wolff muttered to Gunner. "Why's he sending those two amateurs down there? He should have given that mission to you and me."

"As for you, Wolff," Buzz said. "Since you and Jennings screwed up that Brinks robbery, I've got something special in mind for you two cowboys."

Wolff slumped lower in his chair.

"It turns out that you two aren't the only cops who've come up against those armed Mangustas."

That brought Wolff bolt upright again.

"The day before they hit the Brinks car, one of them knocked over a cash pickup at a bank in a shopping mall in East LA. The MO was the same as the Brinks job, but they didn't kill the crew. They just gassed them before they made off with over a million in small bills. No one ID'd the make of the chopper, but it matches your description of the ones you ran into and we're linking them with your robbery."

"Now," Buzz smiled broadly. "Since the LA County PD is not yet equipped with Griffins, they have requested help from Washington in dealing with these bandit gunships, and the request has been approved. And, since we're the Western Region Dragon Flight, we have been given the honor of providing them the gunship support they've requested."

The commander locked eyes with Wolff. "Wolff, Jennings, you two have been placed on temporary duty with the LA County PD to assist them with this problem. You leave tomorrow morning no later than zero seven hundred."

"How long are we going to be there?" Wolff asked.

Buzz smiled. "I guess that depends on you, doesn't it? As soon as you track down those choppers and eliminate them, you can come home." He ignored the look of disgust on Wolff's face. "Any more questions?"

Wolff actually still had quite a few more he wanted to ask, but there was no point in asking them. Not when he was already on top of Buzz's shit list. "No, sir."

"Good," Buzz said. "The movement orders are posted on the board."

* * *

Wolff was not at all pleased when he left the briefing room. Vargas and Simpson were getting the good job this time while he and Gunner were being punished for the Brinks robbery. Flying endless circles in the smog over LA while he waited for someone to call him about a bank robbery in progress was not his idea of a good operation. It was a shit detail if he had ever seen one. But, he smiled to himself, there was an upside to it as well. If the Mangustas were operating in the Los Angeles area, there was a chance that he'd run into them again. And this time he would be damned sure to have plenty of ammunition on board.

"You going to the club for dinner tonight?" Mojo asked when they walked outside the headquarters building.

"Yeah," the pilot answered. "But I'm going to stop off at my room and get a shower first. I had to work all afternoon and I need to change first."

"I'll catch you later," Mugabe said. "I need a beer."

"Keep one cool for me."

CHAPTER 6

TPF Officer's Club, Denver

The Tac Force officer's club was buzzing when Wolff walked in. With the upcoming out-of-town missions, this was the last chance the Dragon Flight cops would have to enjoy their own club for several weeks and the men and women of Dragon Flight were taking full advantage of it. Even though their little club served the same watered-down drinks and overcooked food as did any of the other hundreds of federal officer's clubs across the nation, it was home cooking to them. They would miss it while they were gone, so the club was packed tonight with people risking ptomaine.

After getting a draft beer at the bar, Wolff leaned back and drained a third of it while he scanned the crowd for Mojo. He located him sitting at a table with Gunner and walked over to join them.

"'Bout time you got here," Mugabe said, looking up from the tattered menu he had been trying to decipher. "We were about to start without you."

Wolff pulled back a chair and slid into it. "What's the special tonight?"

"Chicken fried steak," Gunner said, trying hard not to gag.

"Pass." Wolff grimaced with genuine disgust. Some day he was going to serve a federal warrant on the club's cook for his chicken fried steak. What he did to a perfectly innocent piece of meat in the name of southern cooking should be worth at least two years hard time in a federal slammer. "I'll just have a bacon burger and fries."

"But you had that last night," Mugabe reminded him. "You're not eating a balanced diet, Wolfman, and that's not good for you."

"Who the hell do you think you are?" Wolff snapped back. "My mother?"

"Touchy, isn't he?" Gunner said with a big grin.

"Have you also noticed that he gets that way every time someone mentions LA?" Mojo grinned back.

"Who mentioned LA?" Wolff snapped. "I sure as hell didn't."

"Or Reno," Gunner added.

"Speaking of Reno, that was nice fucking work you did down there, Wolfman" came a low, very feminine voice from behind him. "Now I have to go to LA with you and Gunner because you two assholes screwed up again."

Wolff had a big grin on his face as he turned around in his chair to face the tall blond woman wearing a TPF flight suit. "Legs! Nice to see you." His eyes slid up and down her full figure. "How was your day off?"

"I don't want to hear that shit, Wolfman," the blond chopper cop snapped back. "All I want to know is what in the hell you and Gunner thought you were doing running after armed robbers in an unarmed aircraft."

Flight Officer Sandra "Legs" Revell was the co-pilot of Gunner's Dragon One Four and she was not at all happy about having to go to California with the two men. Greater Los Angeles was her least favorite place on the face of the planet.

In the spring of the year 2000, LA was even more

unlivable than it had ever been. The massive state and federal efforts to control air pollution in the Los Angeles basin had failed miserably. Attempts to control traffic had also failed and the feared gridlock had turned LA's freeways into long concrete parking lots. The water supply had finally reached the point where it had to be rationed, and all the palm trees lining the streets had long since died. What little real charm LA had once had was long gone.

Much of LA's business and financial interests had also abandoned the region for the new business centers in Seattle and the Sun Belt states. And, as a result, downtown LA was slowly turning into a massive, sunbaked slum dominated by empty skyscrapers. Some of the outlying suburban areas were still hanging on and the movie industry stubbornly refused to leave Hollywood, but it wouldn't be long before they were forced to shut down and move as well.

All told, LA was a miserable place and Legs wasn't looking forward to spending any more time there than was absolutely necessary.

"Actually, Legs..." Wolff tried to explain. "That whole thing in Reno was Gunner's idea. I was just along for the ride." He nodded in Gunner's direction. "You might want to take this matter up with him."

"And," she said as if she hadn't heard him try to put the blame on her pilot, "I thought I made it clear that I want you to knock off that 'Legs' shit. I'm a little tired of your high-school locker room routine."

"Yes, ma'am," Wolff said, properly subdued. He was beginning to wish that he had never given her that nickname. Every time someone used it, she got on his case about it.

Wolff had spotted Sandra the first day that she had reported for duty at Dragon Flight. A man would have had to have been blind not to have noticed her. There were very few female chopper cops as it was, and none of them looked like her.

He had sauntered up to her with a big grin on his face and had asked her for a date. Trying to make a good first impression, she had patiently explained that she didn't date the men she worked with.

"Great," he had laughed. "Since you're not flying with me, we can have dinner tonight."

She had been sorely tempted by Wolff's boyish good looks, his deep-green eyes, and his easy smile, but she had gone on to explain to him that she was serious about not dating anyone on the force. He had just smiled, slowly running his green eyes up and down her frame.

"Okay Legs," he had said. "I'll catch you later on the flight line."

Wolff's nickname had stuck and so had her determination not to go out with him. It had soon become a ritual with them: every couple of weeks he would ask her for a date and every time she would turn him down. Sandra's rigid rule about not dating the men she worked with was her insurance against finding herself having to work with a man that she no longer wanted to sleep with. Mixing sex and work always made things more complicated and she wanted nothing to distract her from doing her job. And, even though under other circumstances, she probably would have fallen for the dashing pilot's line, she made no exceptions to her rule, not even for the Wolfman.

Sandra had worked hard to get into the Tac Force. She was dead serious about her work and was a tough cop by anybody's standards. She brooked no nonsense from any of the men about being a woman in a "man's" job and backed it up by doing more than her share. She never turned down an assignment, no matter how tough, and she never complained when the men tried to make her lose her temper or quit.

At a statuesque, well-built, five-foot-ten inches and a hundred and forty pounds, she could hold her own in the rough-and-tumble department and often proved it in the hand-to-hand combat training sessions with the men. Anytime she got any shit from one of the male cops, she just patiently waited until the next hand-to-hand class and then calmly proceeded to kick his ass up between his ears. She had not had to do it very often and she had never had to do it twice to the same man.

As a result, Sandra Revell was well respected in Dragon Flight and most of the men she worked with seemed to have forgotten that she was a woman. To them, she was just one hell of a good cop.

Sandra pulled back a chair and took a seat at the table with the men. "How long are we going to be stuck in LA?" she asked.

Wolff grimaced. "Buzz didn't say."

Sandra wasn't put off by his half lie. "Rumor Control has it that he said we couldn't come home until we got those two choppers." She leaned closer to Wolff and smiled tightly. "Is there any truth to that?"

Wolff looked over to Mojo. "Who's in charge of rumor control this week?"

"Goddamnit, Wolff!" she snapped. "What's the story?"

"Well..." Wolff thought fast. "He did say something like that."

"Just exactly what did he say?" Sandra looked from one man to the next.

All three men avoided her eyes.

"That's what I thought." She shook her head. "Jesus H. Christ! What a fuck-up. I wonder if the Southern Region needs a gunner—I've enjoyed about all of you three clowns that I can stand."

"Come on, Sandra," Wolff pleaded. "Give us a break. It's not our fault that Buzz has a royal case of the ass. He's pissed at something and he's just taking it out on us."

"Right."

Just then the waitress appeared, her order pad ready.

"What'll ya have?"

Sandra looked up at her, her jaw tightly clenched. "I'll have a T-bone, rare, and these three assholes will have crow, well done."

The waitress's pencil paused in midair right above the pad. "We don't have that on the menu," she said. "The special tonight is chicken fried steak."

Nobody laughed.

The mercury vapor security lights at the Westside Shopping Center in Rialto, California, cast a warm, golden glow over the parking lot in front of the massive mall structure. Except for a few shadowed areas around the perimeter where the lights had burned out and had not yet been replaced, the parking lot appeared to be empty.

The Rialto patrol car turned into the lot for a closer look; anyway, the two police officers knew better than to trust appearances. There was usually an addict or two shooting up or passed out in front of the barred doorways to the shops, or a derelict who had set up housekeeping in the landscaping.

Rialto was an affluent community, and the citizens prided themselves on living in a clean neighborhood free from most of the problems of the inner cities. They did not allow addicts, bums, and hookers to litter their streets. Since the Chief of Police liked his comfortable job, the town police officers were under strict orders to escort undesirables to the edge of town as soon as they found them.

The passenger in the patrol car reached for the hand mike on the dash clip. "This is Two Boy Four," he radioed to his dispatcher. "We are Code One at the Westside Mall for a mutant roundup."

"Central, copy."

There was also a good chance that the cops would come

upon teenagers screwing in their car. The shadows cast by the row of eucalyptus trees flanking the First Interstate Bank Building at the end of the mall was a favorite make-out spot for the local teenagers. So far tonight, it had been a boring patrol for the two officers. So, after checking the storefronts, the driver turned around to check the area behind the bank. Sneaking up on fornicating teenagers was always good for a couple of laughs.

As they approached the back side of the bank, the driver saw a flash of reflected light. "Looks like we've got young love in the parking lot again," he said, shaking his head. "When are they going to learn that if they want to fuck, they should go somewhere else to do it."

"I hope it's that Williams girl again," his partner grinned. "She's got the finest set of tits in the entire state of California. Maybe even the finest set this side of the Rockies."

"Now I know why you started going to the girls' volleyball games at the school," the driver smiled.

His partner grinned even wider.

The windows of the patrol car were rolled up so the air conditioner didn't have to work overtime to keep out the muggy Southern California smog. Had the windows been rolled down, the officers would have heard the faint whine of a turbine at idle and the whisper of rotor blades set at flat pitch. As it was, they heard nothing.

The officer was driving the car at an idle so as not to startle the young lovers. Part of the routine they followed when they discovered a car parked behind the bank was that they would stop their patrol car short of the parking spot, dismount, grab their Mag Lites, and approach on foot. When they snapped the flashlights on and shined them in the car, they usually got a free sex show.

Sometimes, the kids would be so engrossed in what they were doing that they wouldn't stop till they were done. Other times, there would just be a mad scramble for clothes or the kids would throw the doors open and run panicked into the night. Whatever happened, though, it would brighten up an otherwise dull evening for the two cops.

The patrol car had almost reached the spot where the driver intended to park when a huge, dark shape suddenly rose from the parking lot. "What the fuck!"

The cop riding shotgun snatched the radio mike from the dashboard clip. He had it to his lips and was pressing the push-to-talk switch when a beam of blue light shot out of the center of the dark shape and fastened on their windshield. An instant later, flame blossomed from the side of the shadow and raced for them. The cop didn't even have time to say a word before his world exploded in flame.

A boiling orange-red fireball lit up the parking lot as the patrol car's gas tank exploded. Burning pieces of metal, plastic, and human flesh rained down on the empty parking spaces.

In the light of the burning patrol car, a red Mangusta gunship rose up into the air and quickly disappeared to the south. One of the antitank missile racks on her left stub wing was empty.

CHAPTER 7

TPF Headquarters, Denver

As always, Mugabe was down on the Griffin flight line right as dawn broke over the Mile High City. The day was spring bright, but still a bit cool, a perfect morning for the long flight to Southern California.

Mugabe was always the first to get suited up before a mission. This was a practice he had started back in the good old days when he had first flown for the CIA, the DEA, and anyone else who would give him a mercenary's paycheck to man the weapons from the left-hand seat of a gunship. Being alone at dawn with the sleek, silent gunships always put him in the right frame of mind before a mission. It was his form of meditation, to stand and drink in the silence, knowing that it would soon be gone. In just a few more minutes, the flight line would be full of the chatter of nervous voices, the ringing clang of steel on steel as the weapons were loaded, and the whine or the electric starter motors as the Griffin's turbines were fired up.

For now, however, the co-pilot was alone with his thoughts. Thoughts of the missions he had flown in the past and of the flight they were going to make today.

This thing in LA had all the earmarks of being a real world-class rat fuck. Not that it was going to be all that dangerous, not at all. He was sure that after the first couple of days of inaction, he'd be itching for a chance to fly into a shit-storm just because he was completely bored out of his skull.

The problem with this mission was that it had too high a profile. Every law-enforcement officer and his pet frog would be looking over their shoulders waiting to watch the famed chopper cops go into action. Worse than that was that every California politician up for election this year would be demanding that they do something instantly to stop this helicopter crime wave. It was the sort of thing that would play well on the six o'clock news, and that was bad news for them. Every time they got mixed up in something like this, it always seemed to blow up in their faces.

Mugabe was much more of a chopper gunner than he was a cop. He had started out as a gunner and that was the life he understood best. Putting the cross-hairs on a target and blasting it out of existence was simple and straightforward. The fact that the target often shot back really didn't bother him that much. In fact, it was part of the simplicity of chopper warfare—kill or be killed. The politics of police work, even TPF police work, didn't interest him in the least. And this mission was going to be wall-to-wall politics, both federal and local. No wonder Buzz had his dick in a knot about.

Mugabe looked over and saw Gunner coming out of the maintenance office with a steaming cup of Red's coffee in his hands and shuddered. How in the hell could he stand to drink that shit this early in the morning? Come to think of it, how could he stand to drink it at all. Even when it was fresh, that shit was an environmental contaminant ranking right up there with industrial-grade solvents. Several plans had been hatched in Dragon Flight to report the maintenance chief to the Environmental Protection Agency, but they had all come to naught and Red continued to make his brew. Even knowing that they were shortening their life span, some people continued to drink the stuff.

Mugabe glanced down at his watch. Wolff was going to be late again this morning, but that was not unusual at all. The Wolfman made a fetish out of being fashionably late, but this was not a good morning for it. Buzz still had a waging case of the ass at him and would like nothing more than an excuse to tear his ass off again.

He looked out across the tarmac and saw Wolff finally round the corner of the maintenance building headed for the flight line. As usual, the pilot was still getting dressed as he walked, pulling on his nomex gloves and zipping up his flight suit.

"This is not exactly the best time in the world to be late for takeoff, my man," Mugabe said when Wolff walked up.

The pilot ignored the admonition, his face grim. "You hear the latest?"

Mugabe frowned. "No."

"Those guys with the Mangustas hit right outside of LA again last night," Wolff replied. "This time they knocked over a bank and wiped out a patrol car with an antitank missile in the process. Both cops were killed."

"Jesus."

Wolff shook his head. "The poor bastards didn't even get a chance to get out of their car."

The flight to LA was uneventful, but the news about the bank robbery kept the chopper cops from enjoying it. Even though the Rialto cops had not been Tac Force, the death of any cop was a death in the family. It was a chilling reminder that it could happen to any man or woman wearing a law-enforcement uniform, and that it all too often did.

The LA County Sheriff's Department airfield at Torrance was barely ordered chaos when the two Griffins arrived. The police shared the field with general aviation traffic and it was crowded. The Griffins had to orbit off to the side for quite a while before they received permission from the control tower to land.

Once on the ground, however, things moved a lot smoother. A delegation from the LA County PD welcomed them while their ground crew serviced the two Griffins. After a short briefing on the local situation, the LA operations people outlined a patrol schedule and handed out their radio frequencies and a list of police airfields and facilities.

They were under a great deal of political pressure to stop the Mangustas and wanted the Griffin air cover to start immediately. Legs and Gunner drew the first four hour patrol. With their fuel tanks topped off with JP-4 and their ammunition loads checked yet another time, they taxied out onto the runway and took off into the smog.

While they waited for their turn to go on patrol, Wolff and Mugabe checked out the facilities at the airfield. Since it looked like it was going to be their home for the next several weeks at least, they wanted to know their way around. After being shown the latrines, the pilot ready room, and the canteen, the LA officers wanted to look over the Griffins, so the two chopper cops took them out on the tarmac to show off their machine.

LA County PD was one of four local police departments in the nation that was due to be issued Griffins to form local Dragon Flights and the officers were eager to see what they would be flying later in the year. Wolff was explaining the "Mirror Skin" feature of the Griffin to an attentive audience when a "211 in progress" call came in over the ready-room radio.

"What's a 211?" Wolff asked.

All of the police forces in California used the numbers of the California Penal Code violations as a radio code. The Tac Force, however, always sent information about a crime in clear language so there would be no misunderstanding, and it was going to take them a little time to switch over to the LA system.

"Armed robbery," one of the officers answered as he turned and started for the radio. "It could be your choppers."

"Dragon One Four, this is LA Control" came the voice over Gunner's helmet headphones. "We have a 211 in progress at Whittier Boulevard and Painter in Whittier. Be advised that there are reports of a helicopter gunship at the scene. How copy?"

"LA Control, this is Dragon One Four," Gunner answered as Sandra punched the address into the keyboard of the Griffin's navigational computer. "Good copy, we are Code Zero to that location at this time."

The map of East LA flashed on the navigation screen with a pulsing red location marker centered on a street corner building, the bank that was under attack.

In the left-hand seat of the gunship, Sandra's fingers flew over the controls of her sensors and targeting radar. With all of the electronic background clutter from the densely packed urban area below, it was difficult to filter all of it out so she could get a clear picture of the target area.

Once the sensors were fine-tuned, she flicked the arming switch to the weapons systems. When they were powered up, she dialed in the stun gas round ammo feed for the 40mm grenade launcher and a mix of AP and HE tracer for the 7.62mm chain gun mounted in the nose turret.

The Griffin was capable of being armed with a variety of weapons in its nose turret and on the stub wing weapons pylons. Normally, a 40mm grenade launcher was fitted to the 360-degree turret that could select from a variety of ordnance to include flash-bang grenades, tear gas bombs, smoke cartridges, or a low-fragmentation HE round. A select fire, 7.62mm chain gun was normally mounted beside the grenade launcher. When they needed heavier firepower, the light caliber chain gun could be replaced with a 25mm version that could poke holes in tank armor. But, for what they felt they were up against today, the 7.62mm should be more than enough.

Unlike the earlier electric-motor-driven, multi-barrel Vulcan and mini-gun rapid fire weapons, the chain gun was a single-barrel weapon that could be fired at a variable rate ranging from a single shot to nine hundred rounds per minute. The rate of fire was controlled by the gunner's trigger. A light touch fired a single shot, but pulling all the way back on the trigger unleashed the full power of the weapon.

All of the weapons systems were controlled by the copilot systems operator, but could be fired by the pilot if necessary. As with the sensors, the weapons were slaved to the helmets with the visor serving as the weapons sight as well as providing weapons status data.

As soon as her weapons were armed, Sandra turned to the pilot. "What's the ROE on this operation?" The Tac Force had three levels of Rules of Engagement governing the use of deadly force: the Alpha, Bravo, and Charlie ROE's. ROE Alpha only allowed the use of weapons to save a life, Bravo allowed the Tac Cops to shoot back at anyone who shot at them and Charlie was a shoot-on-sight order that was rarely authorized.

"We're only at Bravo," Gunner replied, his jaw set. True to his nickname, Gunner was not at all pleased about going up against an armed gunship and not being able to blast it out of existence the instant that he laid eyes on it. To give it a chance to shoot first didn't make any sense to him at all. Why give the maggot a chance?

The son of a gunship pilot who had been killed in Vietnam, Jennings tried hard to live up to the memory of the father he had never known. A minor heart murmur had kept him out of the military, but flying a Griffin for the TPF was almost as good as flying combat missions. Particularly when he was going up against another chopper gunship.

"Heads up," Gunner said. "We should be coming up on the target area."

Sandra frowned behind her face mask. "I'm not getting anything," she said, her eyes scanning her sensor readouts. "If there's a chopper somewhere out there, I'm not picking it up. Maybe it's gone already."

Gunner's ears pricked up. This was the same thing Mojo had reported when they closed in on the site of the Brinks robbery. Nothing had showed on the sensors until the Mangustas had been right on top of them. He toyed with the idea that these were some sort of "stealth" choppers, but that was totally absurd. There was no way in hell that a helicopter could hide the radar-return signature of its spinning main rotors. Even though the blades of modern choppers were mostly made from non-metallic composite materials like carbon fiber and plastics, they still reflected radar waves like they were made out of solid steel.

There was simply no such thing as a stealth chopper. The damned thing had to be hiding out of sight behind a building somewhere.

"Keep on 'em," he snapped. "I don't want to get bounced again."

"I still can't see them," she reported.

Gunner had a bad feeling about this situation. Something wasn't right. "Go full defensive," he ordered.

Sandra's fingers flew over her controls. "Defense systems fully activated."

CHAPTER 8

Downtown Whittier

Sandra's going full defensive was the only thing that saved them. When Gunner dropped down lower over the street, the Mangusta jumped out from behind the bank building, its nose turret turning to track the Griffin.

"Look out!" Gunner yelled, stomping down on his rudder pedals to swing his tail around to face the gunship.

In the left-hand seat, Sandra frantically tried to get a radar lock-on for her weapons. For some reason, her target acquisition radar was not tracking the Mangusta. She had it centered in the optical sight on the inside of her face shield, but the red diamond that indicated target lock-on was not showing. "I can't get him!" she yelled.

A puff of dirty white smoke appeared under the right stub wing of the Mangusta. The distance between the two choppers was so short that Gunner didn't even have time to react before the air-to-air missile flashed past them. The Griffin's automatic countermeasures were all that saved them from being blown out of the sky.

When the defensive system had detected the Mangusta's missile IR lock-on, it had started firing decoy flares. The flares burned at over ten thousand degrees and the heat-seeking missile automatically tracked on the flare instead of the cooler turbine exhausts of the Griffin.

Even though she didn't have a target lock-on, Sandra automatically returned fire with the 7.62mm chain gun in the nose turret as Gunner threw the Griffin into a violent evasive maneuver.

Her rounds went wide, but the fire caused the Mangusta to maneuver as it climbed for altitude.

"He's getting away!" Gunner shouted as he threw his ship into position for another shot at it.

Sandra followed the wildly maneuvering Mangusta in her optical sight trying to get a clear shot. The battle had stopped the traffic on the busy streets below and people were looking up at the choppers instead of diving for cover.

"Shoot!" Gunner shouted. "Shoot!"

For an instant, Sandra had the Mangusta centered in the sights and triggered off a short burst. To her horror, she saw her fire miss the gunship and impact on the street. A woman had stopped her car in the middle of the street to see what was going on and was right at the edge of the burst. She took a hit and crumpled to the pavement.

"Oh, shit," Gunner said softly.

"Put it down!" Sandra shouted. "Quick!"

The pilot cut his lift and maneuvered the Griffin down in between the buildings, flaring out for a landing in the middle of the street. Before the Griffin's skids had even touched the pavement, Sandra threw her door open, jumped down, and raced for the woman.

"Quick!" she called back to Gunner as she knelt and tried to staunch the flow of blood from the woman's chest. "Call an ambulance!"

With a single glance after the escaping Mangusta, Gunner keyed his mike. "Control, this is One Four," he radioed. "We need medical assistance ASAP."

* * *

Wolff found Sandra sitting by herself on a bench outside the LAPD radio dispatch office. She was still holding her flight helmet in her hands and her eyes had that empty, thousand-yard gaze usually seen on trauma victims. The blood splattered on her flight suit still looked bright red against the dark-blue nomex.

"You okay, Sandra?"

She looked up at him. "No," she answered honestly. "Not really."

Wolff remembered how shook up she had been in Seattle last year when she had gunned down a Vietnamese teenager. But that had been different. The teenager had been aiming an RPG antitank rocket launcher at one of the Griffins. This time, she had hit an innocent bystander.

"How's the victim?"

"She's still alive," she answered in a low voice. "But she's in intensive care."

"How'd it happen?"

"I don't really know." She shook her head. "When the Mangusta jumped us and started firing, Gunner started maneuvering. I couldn't get a target lock-on and had to shoot with the optical sights. Something happened and I got thrown off target."

Wolff didn't comment. It could have happened to any of them. As long as the chain gun had a target-acquisition radar lock-on, the gun re-aimed itself ten times a second and the target was dead meat. But when you were bare-eyeball shooting and the pilot was maneuvering violently, it was possible to miss.

"What's going to happen now?" she asked him. Wolff couldn't keep his face from looking grim.

"You and Gunner will have to go before a shooting investigation board," he said. "That's the regulation on something like this."

"How soon will that be?"

"Probably in the next couple of days," he replied. "Buzz isn't going to want to let this drag out any longer than necessary. He needs you and Gunner back on duty. And speaking of that," Wolff added, "I don't know if anyone has told you yet, but you and Gunner are also relieved from duty until the board meets. That's also the regulation."

When Buzz learned about the shooting incident, he knew that he would have to be on hand for the investigation. And if he was going to be there, he might as well move his command post to LA. Since all of his force was on assignment in Southern California anyway, it only made sense to move his headquarters there as well. He had never liked trying to run an operation long distance and this was a good reason to get closer to the operation.

"Ruby," he called over his intercom

"Yes, sir?"

"Alert Red and the rest of the staff that we're going to move to jump CP to LA. I want the B Level support crew and staff in place at the airfield by early tomorrow morning."

"Yes, sir."

"And, Ruby," he added, "get me a flight in there as soon as you can this afternoon."

Buzz started scooping up files and reports from his desktop and stuffing them in a bulging briefcase. Why was it always the simplest operations that went tits up? With his force split up the way it was, this was not a good time for something like this to have happened. But, then, there was never a good time for it. Shooting a civilian always meant that someone had not been doing their job.

The news about Gunner and Legs facing a shooting investigation raced through Dragon Flight like wildfire. One of the greatest fears of any police officer was that he might find himself in a situation where he had to use his weapon and an innocent bystander got in the line of fire and was hit.

In actuality, however, few state and local police officers ever fired their weapons in the line of duty. But, when a situation got bad enough for the Tac Force to be called in, it was almost a certainty that their weapons would be used, and mostly sooner than later. That's what the word "tactical" in their name meant; firepower and the ability to deliver it on target.

Fortunately, few civilians had gotten in the way of their operations so far, so shooting investigations were not common in the Tac Force. This would be the first for Dragon Flight and no one ever wanted there to be a second one.

Early the next day it was announced that the shooting board would be headed by a Tac Force Lieutenant Jim Miller from the LA Field Office. Miller had once been a Dragon Flight chopper cop, but he had hung up his TPF pilot's wings when he had taken a job as the Intelligence Officer for the LA field office.

Wolff remembered Miller from the early days of Dragon Flight and he didn't like what he remembered. Miller had always been a little too ambitious and Wolff felt that was a bad sign in a cop. He had taken the job in LA because it carried a promotion with it, and Wolff didn't trust any man who would give up the joy of flying for a ground job. Particularly a desk job on the ground.

Also, Miller was one of those men who never quite fit in with the team, any team. He never hung out with the other off-duty pilots and although he always attended the mandatory unit parties, he always stood off to one aide and never participated in the group grab-ass sessions that always followed the first couple of drinks. He hadn't fit in with the rest of the officers in Dragon Flight and Wolff had not been at all sorry to see him leave.

Sandra was shocked when she learned that Jim Miller

was heading up the investigation board. She, too, had good reason to remember the tall, thin cop, and she didn't have good memories of him, either.

Miller had been her section leader when she had first joined Dragon Flight. From the first day she had been on duty, he had started harassing her. At first it had been only minor things, like making sexual innuendoes every time he was around her. When she didn't respond to those, he had tried to become more than friendly with her and started making small advances toward her. She didn't put up with it, but his ego wouldn't let him take no for an answer.

Miller was more than simply annoying and he made her job more difficult than it really needed to be. But it was not serious enough that she could file an official complaint with Buzz. All she could do was to make sure that she kept out of his way as much as she could.

Then, one night when she was on ramp-alert duty, he caught her alone in the pilot's locker room. He tried to come on to her, apparently under the impression that she would give in to him because he was alone with her. She made it clear that she didn't want anything to do with him, but he paid no attention to her protests and made a clumsy grab for her breasts.

She automatically went into her defensive mode. Her knee came up, slamming into his crotch. He dropped to the floor, clutching his bruised testicles. Without a word, she had turned and walked out of the room leaving Miller behind.

When he left at the end of that week for his new job in LA, she thought that she had seen the last of him. But now he had come back to haunt her like a bad dream. She could only hope that he would not let his earlier experiences with her favor the course of the investigation.

She briefly considered telling Gunner about her run-in with Miller, but she didn't want to sound like a typical whining female using the overworked sexual harassment bit. Miller was a

Tac Force officer and she was confident that he would do the right thing. She couldn't even consider that he might not.

CHAPTER 9

The Federal Building, Los Angeles

Wolff, Gunner, and Mugabe were sitting on the bench outside the hearing room. The board was in its final deliberation after several hours of testimony and only Buzz was allowed to be inside with Sandra. Finally, the door opened and Sandra slowly walked out. Her face was pale, her lips tight as she stared straight ahead.

"Sandra," Wolff said, jumping to his feet.

She walked on past as if she hadn't heard him. When Wolff started after her, Gunner laid a restraining hand on his shoulder. "Let her go," he said.

Buzz stepped out into the hall, his face bleak.

"What happened?" Gunner asked.

The commander looked at his three cops. "They ruled it a bad shooting. She's been suspended pending trial for assault and reckless endangerment."

Gunner's face fell. "You're shitting me! They can't do that! She was defending us. We were under fire, for Christ's sakes!"

Buzz shook his head. "I'm sorry, Daryl," he said. "We'll just have to wait for the outcome of the trial."

"I'll be goddamned if I'm going to wait," the pilot

exploded. "Those sorry motherfuckers…"

"Jennings!" Buzz snapped. "You're a peace officer. You have sworn to uphold the law. And, like it or not, that review board is the law."

Gunner stared at him for a long moment. His right hand slowly went to the left breast pocket of his uniform shirt. He unpinned the gold TPF badge and removed it.

"I'm not a peace officer any longer," he said, handing the badge to his commander. "I just resigned."

He took a deep breath. "I can't belong to any organization that can allow something like this to happen. Legs deserves a fucking medal, not a suspension. Those guys in the Mangusta had us cold and they'd have blown us out of the sky if she hadn't returned fire."

He spun around on his heels and walked down the hall after his co-pilot.

Buzz watched him walk off, his face guarded.

"Jesus," Wolff said softly. "You want me to go after him?"

Buzz thought for a moment. "No, let him get it out of his system. I'll talk to him tomorrow."

"If he shows up tomorrow," Mugabe said, his eyes following Gunner as he walked away. "I've never seen him this pissed off before."

"He's a good cop," Buzz said. "He won't let his personal feelings get in the way of doing his job."

"I wouldn't be too sure about that, sir," Wolff said, looking down the hall after his buddy. "Gunners got his own particular way of looking at things."

"So do I," Buzz said. "But I've got an operation to run here and so do you, so let's get back to it."

As they were about to leave, Lieutenant Jim Miller walked out of the boardroom, a slight smirk tugging at the corners of his mouth. Buzz moved to intercept him. "Miller," he said. "Can I talk to you for a minute?"

"About?" Miller asked curtly, the smirk still on his face.

"About Officer Revell."

"You know that I can't discuss the board's deliberations, Captain," he admonished Buzz. "You'll just have to wait for the report of our findings."

"Come on, Miller," Wolff said, stepping up beside Buzz. "She's one of ours."

"I see you finally made lieutenant," Miller said, emphasizing the word "finally" as his eyes slid up to the rank insignia on Wolff's shirt collar.

Wolff let this jab pass unanswered, but fully planned to take it up with him later.

"And, I see you're still a lieutenant, Miller," Mugabe replied for him. "I thought for sure that you'd be head of the LA Field Office by now."

Miller's cold eyes fixed on Mugabe. "And I see you're still flying around playing cops and robbers. When are you guys going to put a stop to these aerial bank robberies?"

Mojo returned his stare. "Just as soon as you Field Office people get off your dead asses and give us a decent lead we can follow up on."

Miller locked eyes with him for a long moment. "You have everything we have," he said. "You can't expect us to do your work for you."

Without another word, Miller turned away and started down the hallway.

"Whose side is that asshole on anyway?" Wolff asked.

Buzz watched Miller walk away. "In his case, I'd say that he's on his own side."

"Some things never change," Wolff said.

Outside the Federal Building, Gunner squinted against

the sun. There she was just rounding the corner at the end of the block moving at a fast walk.

"Hey, Sandra!" he called out as he took off running after her. "It's Gunner! Wait for me!"

She ignored his call and continued on her way. He followed after her and saw her enter a coffee shop in the middle of the block. He hesitated for an instant, debating whether or not he should go in to her. It was not a difficult decision for him to make. Not only had she been his co-pilot and police partner for several years, she was a woman in trouble.

He took off after her again.

"Sandra?" Gunner said as he walked up to the booth by the window of the cafe. He was puffing from the run down the street. "Can I join you?"

When she looked up at him, Gunner saw that her eyes were dry, but her face was pale and her mouth a tight slit. She nodded curtly and he sat down. She didn't look at him but continued to stare straight ahead, so Gunner didn't attempt to talk to her. He was willing to sit silently while she composed herself.

When the waitress appeared with two cups of coffee and two glazed doughnuts, Gunner laid his Unicard on the table to pay for them, but the waitress handed it back. "First one's on the house," she said.

"Thanks."

Sandra automatically reached for the coffee and took a sip. "It's not as good as Red's," she said softly. Single tears formed in the corners of her eyes and ran unnoticed down her cheeks.

Gunner turned his eyes away, not wanting to embarrass her by noticing the involuntary tears. The pilot had known Sandra both on and off duty for a long time. He had seen her stressed out, he had seen her under fire, he had seen her hurt, and he had seen her kill. He had seen his copilot under circumstances that most men never see women, even their wives. But he had never seen her lose her legendary self-control before.

Her two tears disturbed him in a way he could not even begin to put into words.

Daryl Jennings was not a complicated man. He had a simplistic, almost naive, view of the world that was clearly defined in colors of pure black and white. There were no shades of gray in the world according to Gunner. This was not necessarily a bad attitude for a cop to have, except when it came to his dealings with the women in his life. Particularly the police women.

Before meeting Sandra, Gunner had believed that all women were good for only one thing, including women cops. He had treated them all the same and they had responded to him according to their own needs and desires. Regardless of the widely held belief that American women had somehow changed in the last thirty years, there were still more than enough of them around who wanted to be treated as having only one role in life. Therefore, Gunner was never without feminine companionship for very long.

When he had first started working with Sandra, he had naturally tried that approach with her. Unlike the women he was used to, however, Sandra wasn't flattered. In fact, she immediately kicked his ass up between his ears.

That incident began a long-overdue period of education about modern American women for Gunner Jennings.

In the three years since then, he had flown countless hours with Sandra in the left-hand seat of his Griffin, manning the ship's weapons and sensors. And, to his complete amazement, he had discovered that she was as good a cop as any man. In fact, she was better than most of the men he had worked with, and he had freely trusted his life to her on more than one occasion.

This revelation put Gunner in a difficult position. He couldn't put the make on her because she'd break him in two, but even though she was the best cop he had ever worked with, she was still a woman. Gunner solved this dilemma with his typical simplistic view of the world. In his mind, Sandra became an honorary man.

That had solved many of the problems he had working with her on a daily basis, but this crisis was something he had not encountered before. There was something about seeing her grimly fighting back her tears that made him feel very protective of her. He almost felt the way he did when one of his girlfriends cried, and this confused him. He wasn't confused, however, about what he thought about the whole fucking mess. He was pissed.

"Sandra," he said. "They shouldn't have done that to you. It's not right."

She looked at him and tried to smile. "They have their job to do."

"Bullshit!" he exploded. "They've got no fucking right to suspend you for something like that. It was an accident, pure and simple. If that old bitch had had any brains, she wouldn't have gotten hit. Jesus H. Christ! No one in their right fucking mind stops their car in the middle of a fire fight to see what's going on."

"I should have been more careful."

"If you had hesitated, we'd have died," he stated flatly. "That guy had us cold. You saved our lives again."

Her eyes noticed the bare spot on the left breast of his uniform shirt. "Where's your badge?"

He locked eyes with her. "I gave the goddamned thing back to Buzz."

She was stunned. Now her mistake was affecting him, too. "You didn't have to do that, Gunner."

His eyes blazed. "The hell I didn't," he snapped. "I'm not about to work for an organization that can do something like that to you."

He realized that his statement sounded suspiciously like he had a personal interest in her and he quickly rephrased it. "To you or to any one of the other guys, either."

Sandra was silent, not knowing what to say. She had known for years that Gunner saw her as more than just his police partner. But, ever since she had laid out the ground rules to him in the hand-to-hand training room, he had been very careful not to give her any sign that he was interested in her as a woman. Now, however, her situation was making him overly protective of her. She wasn't used to this kind of treatment from him and wasn't sure how she should respond.

"Gunner..." she started to say. "You shouldn't have done..."

"No, damnit!" He shook his head. "I'm serious. I'm not going to put that badge back on till you've been reinstated with a clean record."

She knew enough about her pilot to know that there was little chance of him changing his mind once he had set upon a course of action. People who called Gunner hardheaded were understating the case, badly understating it.

"What are you going to do till the trial?" he asked, changing the subject.

"I thought I'd stay in LA, in case they need to contact me again before the hearing."

Gunner thought carefully for a moment. "I'll tell you what," he said brightly. "Why don't you and I get us a room in the same motel. That way I can be there if you need help with something."

"But you've got to fly."

He smiled grimly. "You forget that I resigned. I don't ever have to fly again unless I want to."

She looked at him, a mixture of relief and sadness in her face. "You really don't have to do this for me," she said.

"Forget it," he said. "I've done it."

CHAPTER 10

Torrance Airfield, Los Angeles

The results of the Internal Affairs Board inquiry into Sandra's shooting incident sent Dragon Flight into a tailspin. This was the first time in the history of the Tac Force that one of their members had been suspended for a bad shooting and it affected every man and woman in TPF blue.

Dragon Flight used up more ammunition in the defense of the law than most state police forces used on the firing range, and it had only been a matter of time before one of those rounds found the wrong target. Nonetheless, it was still a shock for the chopper cops to have had one of their own judged to have committed a bad shooting, and Buzz had his hands full dealing with a major morale problem.

Had it been one of the men who had been caught up in this, it still would have been bad. But to have had the best female cop in federal service suspended made it twice as bad. And that was without taking into consideration Gunner's totally unexpected resignation. As a man, Buzz understood Gunner's feelings, but as a cop, he knew that personal feelings had to be put aside in the line of duty. And as a Dragon Flight commander, Gunner's personal feelings had completely screwed up an already overly complicated operation. The first thing Buzz had to do was to find a replacement crew for Dragon One Four so he could meet his commitments. And he knew that was not going to be easy to do. All of the four Tac Force regions had their hands full right now. Springtime always brought out the worst in some people.

It was times like this that made him wonder if he had been wearing a police uniform too long. Normal Tac Force operations were bad enough, but to have to try to deal with something like this in the middle of a split operation away from their home base was more than he wanted to have to put up with. If he made it through this mess, he just might take advantage of the TPF early retirement program and go fishing for a year or two in Alaska.

He reached for the intercom button on his desk. "Ruby," he said when Mom answered, "can you put me through to the Southern Region Commander?"

"Yes, sir," Mom snapped back.

Jesus, Buzz thought, everyone's got their guts in an uproar today. Screw 'em, though, they all had jobs to do the same as he did, and if he had his feet in the fire, then their toes would be getting warm, too.

After calling in all his markers, he finally talked the Southern Region commander out of a replacement Griffin crew, but it would be a couple of days until they could arrive. In the meantime, he had no choice but to double up on the bank patrols and have Wolff and Mugabe be on call twenty-four hours a day. The two Griffins working with the DEA had priority and he couldn't pull one of them back from that assignment to cover for Gunner.

"Ruby?" he called again. "Can you put me through to the pilots' lounge? I need to talk to Wolff or Mugabe."

Wolff was not at all pleased that he and Mugabe had been

put on twenty-four-hour duty. Not only did it mean hours of butt-numbing flying in endless circles around in the smog, but it also meant that he and Mojo wouldn't get a chance to sample what little LA had left in the way of night life. Not only did he and his gunner share their off-duty enjoyment of messing around with old flying machines, they also shared another hobby as well—women.

As far as Wolff was concerned, one of the biggest perks of being a TPF chopper cop was that he got to spend most of his time away from the Denver home base. This gave him a wide area to pursue his other off-duty passion. And, as with their playing with the Corsair together, Mugabe was never far away when Wolff went bar-hopping and skirt-chasing. This assignment, however, didn't look like it was going to provide much in the way of evening entertainment—Not if they were going to have to be available to fly twenty-four hours a day.

He went to find Mugabe to give him the good news.

The black gunner was over in the small hangar that had been taken over by Red and a skeleton staff of mechanics that Buzz had had flown in from Denver. Now that the maintenance people had moved in, Torrance Airfield was starting to feel like a real Dragon Flight operation. Wolff always felt more comfortable when he was working with his own gang, and hearing Red yell at some poor unfortunate as he walked up made California almost feel like home.

In fact, the only thing missing from Dragon Flight's new home right now was Gunner and Legs. Wolff had never realized how much he would miss those two until now. And he missed them for more than just the work they would have taken off his back had they been available for duty. It just wasn't the same without having Legs and Gunner around to harass.

Mojo turned around when Wolff walked into the hangar, a frown on his face. "What's the story on the revised flight schedule?"

Wolff shook his head. "Buzz can't get a replacement crew in right away, so we're on a twenty-four-hour standby till they can get here."

Mugabe shook his head. "What a fucking mess. We're never going to catch those guys by ourselves. There's just no fucking way we can cover an area as big as LA with only one Griffin. We'll be stuck down here forever if we don't get some help with this."

"Buzz says that they'll be here in three days max."

"So for the next seventy-two hours the only thing standing between two renegade chopper gunships and the security of greater LA is us."

"That's about it."

"God help LA."

"The good news is that instead of flying around in the sky all day, we're to stay here on ramp alert."

Mugabe wiped his hands on a dirty rag. "We'd better see about getting bedded down somewhere then."

"Let's go check with the locals and see if they can help us find a place to sleep."

Since there were no billeting facilities at the airfield, the LA officers set up cots for Wolff and Mugabe in the back of their locker room for the duration. The rest of the Dragon Flight personnel had been given rooms in a nearby motel, but since Wolff and Mojo were on ramp alert, they couldn't even go across the street to sleep.

"Home sweet home," Mugabe announced as he unpacked his flight bag into one of the empty lockers.

"This is bullshit," Wolff said. "There's no way in hell that we can cover this city with one Griffin. We couldn't even do it with all four ships."

"Tell that to Buzz."

"I did, and he told me that he was sure that a couple of ace flyers like us should be able to handle it."

"How long is he going to stay pissed off at us about the Reno thing?"

"Beats the shit outta me," Wolff shrugged. "But I'm getting a little tired of the treatment."

"Why don't you go talk to Mom," Mugabe suggested. "Maybe she knows what's eating him."

"Good idea."

Buzz's command post had been set up beside the hangar, so after putting his things away, Wolff walked over to have a little chat with Mom. When anyone needed to know what was really going on with Dragon Flight, she was the only one who would really know. He found her at her duty station, the communications console, wearing the headset that put her in instant radio and computer contact with the outside world. "Hi, Mom," he said with a smile.

"What do you want, Wolfman?"

"Nice talk," he said. "I come over to talk to you and that's all you can say to me?"

"I'm busy, what do you want," she repeated. "What's the story on that replacement crew?" he asked. "When are they coming in?"

"When did Buzz tell you they were coming?"

"Come on, Mom," he pleaded. "Gimme a break. I need to know. Mojo and I are stuck with pulling twenty-four on and none off till they get here."

"That sounds like a personal problem to me."

It was obvious to Wolff that he wasn't going to get any sympathy from her today. "Okay," he said. "But can you tell me what in the hell is eating Buzz? He's been on my ass for the last several days now."

Ruby turned in her chair to face the pilot. "You want to know what's wrong with the captain? Is that it?"

Wolff nodded.

"Where do you want me to start? With that beautiful job

you did in Reno? Or with the flak he's taking from Washington about those Mangustas? Or maybe I can tell you how he's feeling about Legs getting suspended. What in the hell's wrong with you, Wolfman? Get your head out of your anal cavity and get back to work."

Wolff leaned over and brushed his lips past Ruby's hair. "I love you too, Mom," he said.

"Get the hell outta here," she growled. "If you're not flying, get your young ass down to the flight line and give Red a hand."

Wolff straightened up and saluted. "Yes, ma'am."

"Wiseass."

"Did you get anything out of Mom?" Mojo asked when Wolff got back to the hangar.

"It must be that time of month for her, too," the pilot answered. "Everyone's gone nuts around here."

"Maybe it's the pollution." Mojo looked up into the brownish sky.

Wolff shrugged. "All I know is that I'd sure as hell like to get this thing wrapped up and go home. This place is bad news for us."

"Speaking of bad news," Mojo looked over Wolff's shoulder. "Here comes Red and he doesn't look happy."

"What's new about that? He's always had a permanent case of the ass."

"Wolff, Mojo?" Red said. "I just heard that One Zero has been put on twenty-four-hour alert."

"That's what the man said," Wolff answered.

"How in the hell am I going to pull the scheduled maintenance on that ship? It's past due to have the igniters gone over."

"Beats me," Wolff said. "Maybe you'd better talk to Buzz

78

about that."

"Look, can I talk you guys into flying One Four while I work on One Zero?"

Wolff really didn't like to fly anybody else's chopper. Even though all of the Griffins were as identical as modern technology could make them, he still felt that One Zero was somehow special, a cut above her sisters. He had flown that ship for so long that it seemed to answer his thoughts more than it did his control movements. He knew, however, that this was not the best time in the world to say something like that to Red.

"Sure," he said. "I don't see any problem with that. Just as long as it's not going to take all week."

Red looked relieved. He knew how pilots felt about their favorite ships. "Don't worry, we'll get her back to you as fast as we can."

"Get your guys to mount my seat in One Four first," Wolff added. "I can't park my ass for hours in that same skinny little seat that Gunner uses. My legs will fall asleep."

"Change mine, too," Mojo said. "Legs is twice as broad across the ass as I am."

The Griffin's armored seats came in three different sizes to accommodate different body sizes. And there was nothing quite as bad as having to fly for hours in a seat that wasn't the right size.

"We'll get right on it," Red promised.

"I'll go check out the armament and sensor systems, too," Mojo said. "No one's looked at them since Gunner and Legs tangled with that Mangusta."

CHAPTER 11

Downtown Los Angeles

By the third day of her forced inactivity, Sandra Revell was ready to climb the faded walls of her second-rate motel room. For the last two days she had laid around, slept, watched too much TV, wandered the city, walked the beaches, and generally tried to keep from thinking. It wasn't working, however, and the inactivity was driving her to despair. One of the things that made Sandra such a good cop was the high energy level that she brought to her work. Being a chopper cop was her life. And without it to fill her time, she simply didn't know what to do with herself.

When she awoke that morning, she didn't know what she was going to do with that day, much less what she would do to fill the time during the two weeks before her first court appearance. She had been on the phone to her defense lawyer a couple of times, but there was little else she could do to fight for herself until after the arraignment.

She hurriedly dressed, but then stood and stared out of the dirty window at the traffic on the streets below. There had to be something else that she could do other than just lie around and wait for the ax to fall. She had never been very good at waiting.

She reached for the phone on the bed stand and called

over to Gunner's room. He had taken the room next to hers in case she needed help, as he had put it. And, since he had offered, maybe there was something he could do for her.

"Gunner," she said when he picked up the phone.

"This is Legs, let's go get some breakfast."

"Sure," he said. "Be right over."

For the last two days, Gunner had stuck to Sandra like a shadow. He hadn't intruded on her solitude, but had kept in the background patiently waiting to see if there was anything he could do for her. As yet, beyond having dinner with her, there had been little he could do, and the inactivity was weighing on him as well. He smiled as he put down the phone receiver. She had just called herself Legs. That meant that she was back for duty and he wondered what she had in mind.

The coffee at the Denny's restaurant across the street from the motel was a Class A Felony, but it was the closest place to meet and she was waiting for him when he arrived. As he walked up to the booth, he noticed that she wore a slight smile on her face. That was something he hadn't seen since the shooting and it was a welcome sight.

"Yo, Legs," he said. "How're you doing?"

She ignored his question. "We need to talk."

"'Bout what?"

Her smile widened. "I've got a hell of an idea."

"What's that?"

Just then the waitress appeared and Sandra clammed up until she had taken their orders. As soon as the waitress turned her back, Sandra leaned over the table. "I want you to go undercover with me."

"What!" Gunner didn't want to believe that he had heard her correctly. "We're not packing badges anymore, remember?"

"I know that, damnit!" she shot back. "But we still know the drill. I want to get out there and find out who in the hell's behind those Mangustas."

She leaned back against the bench. "The way I look at it, if we can find them, they'll be charged with causing the shooting and that'll take some of the heat off me."

Gunner thought for a moment. Sure, they were both ex-cops. But they were chopper cops, not street cops, and undercover work was not the sort of thing you could do from the cockpit of a Griffin. But she did have a point. They had both heard enough war stories about undercover street work from the TPF field office people that they should be able to pull it off. "That's not a bad idea," he said. "Exactly what did you have in mind?"

"Well..." she said. "I was thinking that you could pose as a drug dealer and I would be your girlfriend."

Gunner had to bite back a laugh. Sandra Revell a street pusher's main squeeze? Not bloody likely. Anyone looking at her would see in an instant that she had far too much class to get caught up in that kind of dead-end shit. Even so, though, he had to admit that the idea had merit.

"The way I figure it," she continued, "someone on the street has got to know where those Mangustas are operating from. And, if we can find that out, we can track those bastards down."

"But, why the drug dealer scam?" he asked.

"Well," she said. "I was trying to figure out what's behind all of this. It takes a pretty big organization to be able to afford to operate not only one, but at least two, million-dollar helicopter gunships. Think about it. They've got to have an airfield somewhere, maintenance facilities, fuel, ammunition, and everything else that goes with it. This is not some nickel-and-dime operation run by your usual small-time street maggots. This is big time, real big time."

"You've got a point there," Gunner admitted. "And big organizations are into drugs. The bigger the organization, the more they're into them."

"But then, why knock off banks?" Gunner pointed out the only flaw in her reasoning. "Big organizations don't do things like that. Robbing banks is street-maggot action, not big time."

She stared at her coffee cup for a moment. "Maybe they're knocking over banks to finance their drug operations. Didn't Buzz say that this new stuff, what did he call it, 'edge'? Is being sold at a real low street price? What if the same guys who are behind the bank jobs are also the guys who are pushing 'edge'?"

"Jesus, Legs," Gunner said with a frown. "Isn't that a real long shot? I mean," he added when he saw the look on her face, "I want to get to the bottom of this, too, believe me. But don't you think that's a little far out?"

She looked thoughtful for a moment. "No," she said slowly. "In fact, the more I think about it, the more it makes sense to me. Real good sense."

Gunner knew that he wasn't a rocket scientist and he was honest enough with himself to know that Sandra was a heck of a lot smarter than the average woman he usually ran around with. Maybe she was on to something here. Maybe it was worth looking into. At least it sure beat the hell out of sitting around in a dingy motel room.

"Okay," he said, his face breaking into a smile. "How do you want to work this?"

Actually, Sandra Revell was not too far off the mark. The Mangustas were being operated by a large crime organization. But it wasn't an organization that she really knew anything about. And she had missed the mark about them being the ones who were pushing 'edge' on the streets. They weren't pushing it, they were the ones who were manufacturing it. They left the distribution of the new drug up to a small army that had been recruited specifically for that purpose. That way, if a pusher was caught, he wouldn't know anything about his bosses. The only guys he could turn in was the midlevel distributor who was also a freelancer with no real knowledge of the supplier's operation.

This was a classic "Cut Out" operation and could only have been put together by an experienced organization with a great deal of money to put into it. An organization like the Italian Mafia. And not the watered-down American versions of the Mafia, either. This operation was being run by the old-fashioned Sicilian crime organization with a little help from the French syndicate.

As Buzz had said in his briefing, 'edge' was a designer drug, but it had not been designed on purpose. 'Edge' was an accident that had been discovered by an Italian chemist working to improve the French RU-486 abortion pill. RU-486 had been discovered in the late eighties and by the mid-nineties it was the only hope to hold back the uncontrolled population growth in developing countries.

Resistance from the religious right and the liability lawyers in the United States had prevented any American pharmaceutical companies from producing the drug, but they had not been able to keep it from being imported. To supply the demand in the United States, an Italian company had acquired licensing rights from the parent French company and was producing millions of the pills in a modern factory just south of the California border in Tijuana, Mexico.

The Mexican government welcomed the factory, not only for the jobs and tax revenue it provided, but because it provided a cheap source for the abortion pills. Mexico City had long since passed Tokyo and Calcutta to become the world's most populated city, and the government was frantically trying anything it could to keep the birth rate down. What the Mexican authorities did not know, however, was that the factory was owned and operated by the Italian Mafia.

Large crime organizations had learned long ago that there

was actually far more money to be made in legal business than there was in crime. In fact, many businesses were nothing more than legalized criminal activities so it made more sense to go legit rather than put up with the constant hassles from the police and prosecutors.

When the Cold War ended in Europe in the early nineties, it had been the criminal organizations who had been among the first westerners to go into the recently freed Eastern European nations with offers of investment money. It had been a great way to launder crime money, and from there it had been easy for them to go into manufacturing and particularly pharmaceutical manufacturing. After all, they had made their money with drugs and they knew the business well.

An Italian chemist working in the laboratory of the Mexican factory had been looking for a way to combat depression, one of the side effects of RU-486, when he stumbled onto the combination of chemicals now known as 'edge'.

When preliminary testing showed that the compound not only combated depression, but also gave the user an artificially heightened feeling of both mental and physical power, they knew that they had a winner on their hands. The fact that the drug was highly addictive only added to its value...

But not as a legitimate pharmaceutical—rather as a new street drug.

And, since the factory's owners knew street drugs better than they did the pharmaceutical ones, it didn't take them long to decide to put 'edge' into production and build a distribution network. But, rather than operate like the rest of the crime organizations behind street drugs did, they decided to go into business with 'edge' in a business-like manner. That required capital and that was where the Mangustas came in.

The Augusta Aerospace AA-149 Mangusta II was the hottest of the Euro-defense attack choppers. The product of an Italian aerospace firm, loaded with Israeli weapons systems and

German electronics, it was the premier gunship chopper in the world, edging out even the American's new AHX-I Geronimo. It was fast, it was hard-hitting, and it was expensive. So expensive in fact that few armies could afford to fly it except for, of course, the Israeli and German armies.

But the Augusta Aerospace Mangusta manufacturing facility employed several people from the same Mafia family that owned the RU-486 factory in Mexico. Therefore, it had not been difficult for them to designate two Mangusta II airframes just coming off of the production lines as static test vehicles and then test them to destruction. Except that the two wrecks that were written off were actually two test machines left over from the original test program. The two new airframes were secretly outfitted and freighted to a remote port in the Yucatan of Mexico where they were off-loaded.

After flight testing, the two choppers had been fitted with a special electronics package and flown to a remote airfield in northern Mexico. From there, they ranged out to hit banks and armored cars.

Sandra's hunch had been right on. With the Mexican government keeping a close watch on the finances of the RU-486 factory for tax purposes, it was difficult to find the money to finance the startup of the 'edge' production line and the distribution network. As with all business, there were costs involved with any new product. Particularly a product that had so much competition, such as a recreational drug.

To build a decent market share on the streets, 'edge' was being sold far below its actual production costs. It was expensive to do business that way, but in the long run, it was certain to pay off. But, until the user base could be built, the production had to be paid for somehow. And if a profit could be made at the same time, so much the better.

CHAPTER 12

High Over Los Angeles

Wolff and Mugabe were flying through the smog blanketing LA at five thousand feet. Any higher than that, and they would not have been able to see the city sprawled out below them. As it was, even that high up it was difficult to pick out details. But, for the most part, that was a blessing. It was sad to see the slum that LA had become.

In the year 2000, most Americans were used to seeing New York and the other major East Coast cities in ruins. They had been going steadily downhill for decades, and no one really cared if they looked like a war zone. But LA had always had a special charm: part affluence, part climate, and part sheer size. For as long as anyone remembered, LA had been the great American dream city where anything was possible if you worked hard enough. And it had remained that way until the late 1990's. LA had always had its problems, every major city had problems, but they had always been workable problems. For some reason, however, the problems suddenly went from bad to worse all at once. The chronic shortage of fresh water, the impossible traffic, the Byzantine, corrupt local politics, the blanket of smog that not even most rigid emission controls in the world could handle, the unstoppable swarm of illegal immigrants from south of the border, and a crime rate that was unmatched by even Mexico City suddenly became too much for most people to deal with.

Actually, the quality of life in LA had been unbearable for several years, but the residents had kept trying to make a silk purse out of a sow's ear. Suddenly, though, like a new infectious disease sweeping through the area, all at once the local inhabitants stopped even trying to make it work. Within a two-year period, anyone who could afford to leave LA had left. And now, the hard corps stay-behind residents were desperately struggling to revive the corpse of the once-great city. But LA resembled a poorly run, third-world nation rapidly going downhill.

It was particularly sad for Wolff to see LA falling apart this way. He had spent some of the best years of his life in LA shortly after he had been thrown out of the Air Force Academy and before he became a chopper cop. Back then, not even the sky had been a limit to a younger Rick Wolff with a pilot's license in his back pocket and a steady willingness to fly anything with wings or rotors. He had started his aerobatic and air-racing career back then, flying for anyone who needed a pilot with nerves of steel and a soft touch on the controls.

In fact, it had been his years in LA that had shown Wolff the need for a more effective police force. Even back then, LA had started sliding sharply into chaos, and seeing what crime was doing to his adopted hometown had made him decide to try to become part of the Tac Force, the nation's elite law enforcement agency. Now, however, LA was no longer a place where he wanted to be. In fact, it was now one of his worst nightmares; being a cop, but being totally unable to do anything to stop the most blatant crime. Even with the awesome power of the Tac Force behind him, he couldn't stop an armed helicopter gang from robbing banks.

Yesterday, the Mangusta had struck again, hitting another armored car cash shipment. This was the fourth aerial robbery in a little over a week and Washington was going crazy. Since California was still the nation's most populated state, the state's congressional delegation had a great deal of power on Capitol Hill and they were using all of it on this case. Not only was the replacement crew for Gunner's ship coming in tomorrow, but two more Griffins were being transferred in for temporary duty until this crisis was ended.

The problem, however, was that with even more Griffins in the air, they were still no closer to learning who was behind this than they had been when they had started. The LA Field Office had not been able to give them any leads, and flying around in the sky in hopes that they would accidentally bump into the Mangustas bordered on the absurd. But it calmed the local politicians, and it was all they could do until they got a lead.

Wolff had even talked Buzz into asking the Air Force to use the KH series spy satellites to make recon photo runs over the entirety of Southern California in hopes of spotting the Mangustas. But so far, nothing had shown up on the high-resolution photographs. The cameras on the KH birds could read a newspaper headline in Moscow from 250 miles in space, but the smog was so thick in LA that they were lucky to even be able to pick up a newspaper truck, much less a newspaper.

"I've got to have Red adjust these rudder pedals again," Wolff growled. "They're still too fucking close."

Flying Gunner's Dragon One Four was doing nothing to brighten Wolff's day. Gunner had adjusted all of the control feedbacks to suit him, which made them too heavy for Wolff, who flew with a lighter, more gentle touch. "And this thing still flies like a fucking truck."

Mojo wasn't having any better luck with Sandra's weapons and sensor console, either. It had taken him most of the morning to adjust them to the sensitivity that he was accustomed to working with, but they still didn't feel the same. It was like wearing someone else's underwear. He was covered, but it just didn't feel quite right.

"Give it a couple more hours," the gunner said. "You'll get used to it."

"No wonder I've always been able to fly circles around him," Wolff muttered. "He should have been a fucking Greyhound bus driver."

"Dragon One Zero, this is Dragon Control," Mom's voice came in over Wolff's headphones.

"One Zero, go."

"This is Control, we have a 211 in progress, eighteen hundred block of Ocean Boulevard in Long Beach. Respond Code Zero. How copy?"

"One Zero, good copy," Wolff replied as Mugabe's fingers punched in the address. "Going Code Zero."

As he banked his machine over to take up the new flight heading, and twisted the throttle up against the stop, he glanced down at the screen showing the location of the robbery. "Echo Tango Alpha eight minutes."

"Control, copy," Mom replied. "Be advised that an armed helicopter is reported at that location."

"Good copy."

Mojo flicked on the switches for the turret weapon's controls and dialed in a mix of high explosive and armor-piercing tracer 7.62mm ammunition for the chain gun. He switched the 40mm ammunition feed for the grenade launcher over to straight high-explosive rounds. If he got a chance to pull the trigger on that Mangusta, he wanted to make sure that he could take it out with the first burst.

Mom was back on the air in a few seconds. "This is Control, be advised that your target has landed beside a warehouse and has fired on the security guards."

"One Zero, copy. What's in the warehouses?"

"We do not have that information at this time."

"One Zero, copy. We'll be there in six and find out ourselves."

"Control out."

As Wolff and Mugabe approached the location, they were just in time to see the angular shape of a Mangusta lift out of the parking lot next to a large building. The gunship kept close to the ground as it swiftly banked and raced for the south, giving up altitude for airspeed.

"There he is!" Mojo shouted.

"I've got him," Wolff replied as he dropped down lower to take up the pursuit.

But, even with the two GE turbines screaming at 110 percent RPM, Wolff was not catching up with the Mangusta. He flattened the pitch on his main rotors even more to decrease the drag. It cut his lift, but at this speed, the turbine exhausts were providing most of his forward thrust and the stub wings most of the lift.

He was flying One Four faster than the designers had ever intended a Griffin to fly, but it still wasn't fast enough. He couldn't gain on the bastard. He hunched over the controls as if willing the machine to try even harder. Now was the time that he really missed not being behind the controls of One Zero. He was sure that he could have squeezed a few more miles an hour out of his own ship.

"Can you hit him from here?" he asked Mojo.

Mojo looked up from his weapon's sight. "Not yet. Get in closer."

"I'm trying, I'm trying!"

Half a mile in front of the speeding Mangusta, a plume of thick black smoke filled the air. Someone had set an abandoned apartment block on fire. Burning buildings were so common in the deserted sections of LA that the fire department didn't even bother to respond to the alarms anymore. It was better for all concerned if the ruins burned to the ground. Banking away to the right, the red gunship headed straight for the thick pall of smoke.

"He's getting away," Mojo said grimly, his finger itching to squeeze the trigger for the chain gun, but the Mangusta was still completely out of range for the 7.62mm mounted in the turret today. If they had been carrying the optional, heavier 25mm version of the chain gun, he would have had a chance. But the lighter 7.62mm just wouldn't reach out far enough.

"I've got him," Wolff said as the Mangusta disappeared into the smoke. "I've got him."

A few seconds later, Wolff throttled back as he dove into the blinding smoke guiding on his terrain-following radar. "Where's he going?"

"I don't know." Mojo's hands flew over the sensor controls. "I've lost him."

Wolff broke out into clear air. Twisting his throttle all the way against the stop and hitting the over-rev switch again, he scanned the sky looking in vain for the red gunship. It was nowhere in sight. "Goddamnit! He can't have disappeared again. Where the fuck is he?"

Mojo looked over at the pilot, a look of bewilderment visible behind his face shield. "He's gone, the screen's completely empty."

"Jesus Christ, Mojo." Wolff sounded disgusted. "What the fuck's wrong with you? We were right behind him. How the hell did you lose him?"

"I never had a lock on him," Mojo admitted. "The radar isn't working. I was tracking him optimally while I tried to get a lock-on."

"Ah, shit," Wolff shook his head as he chopped his throttle. "Buzz is going to have our asses in a sling for this."

Wolff was thoroughly pissed off when he stepped down out of the cockpit of One Four at Torrance Airfield. Mojo wasn't feeling any better, either. In fact, he was probably even more pissed off than his pilot.

The two of them stormed into Red's office loaded for bear, red bear. "Red!" Wolff called out when he spotted the maintenance chief bent over a box of spare parts. "I need to talk to you. Now!"

Red straightened up, a boxed turbine oil filter in his hand, and paused to make a check on his parts stock list. "I'm busy right now."

"You're not half as busy as you're going to be in a second if you don't talk to me," Wolff warned, his fists clenched at his side.

Red put the part down and shifted his dead cigar to the other side of his mouth. "It's your nickel."

"I need One Zero back and I need it right now."

"What's wrong with One Four?"

"It flies like a fucking tank," Wolff snapped. "No wonder Gunner never could keep up with me in the air. That thing's a piece of shit."

Red took a deep breath. No one criticized his Griffins, no one, not even Rick Wolff. He opened his mouth to speak, but Mojo broke in before he could say a word. "And the sensors don't work worth a shit, either," he said quietly. "I couldn't get a lock on the target. Radar, IR, nothing."

Red shut his mouth. Wolff bitched all the time, but Mojo only bitched about the equipment when he had something important to say. "Okay," he said patiently. "What happened out there today?"

Wolff and Mojo quickly recounted their latest encounter with the Mangusta. Red took it all in carefully, but it sounded to him like the two fliers had fucked up again somehow. "Look, guys," he said. "Go ahead and write it all up. I'll go over it later."

"How about One Zero?" Wolff asked.

"She's almost ready," Red said. "You can have her back

in a couple of hours."

"'Bout time," Wolf growled as he turned around and stomped out of the office.

Red chewed thoughtfully on his dead cigar as he watched the pilot go. He almost felt sorry for Wolff; he thoroughly understood his frustration. But then, this place had everyone on edge. He, for one, would be very glad when this whole mess was over. He walked over to his ever-brewing coffeepot, poured another cup of the vile brew, and went back to his parts inventory.

Fuck-ups or not, he still had to keep track of his spares. As long as the Griffins were flying, somebody had to keep them in the air.

CHAPTER 13

Torrance Airfield, Los Angeles

In the furor created by the aftermath of the Legs and Gunner shooting investigation, the after-action report they had written on the incident had been completely forgotten. No one was aware that they had not been able to pick up the subject Mangusta on their radar or sensors until it had been right on top of them. No one had taken notice of Gunner's "stealth chopper" comment or had thought to compare it with Wolff's report from the Brinks job that had mentioned the same thing having happened there.

It wasn't until Wolff and Mugabe were unable to keep track of the chopper that had pulled the raid on the warehouse in Long Beach that anyone realized there was something out of the ordinary about the two renegade Mangustas.

And, actually, it was an intelligence specialist, a tech weenie at the Denver Headquarters who finally put two and two together and came up with "wait a minute!"

There wasn't any such thing as stealth choppers; it was a scientific impossibility. Therefore, the problem had to be an equipment malfunction on the Griffins.

The specialist put a priority buck slip on the report and immediately shot it back to the mobile Dragon Flight

95

headquarters in LA for action. In short, the note went over the evidence for the stealth chopper theory, debunked it, and ordered Red to check all of the sensor equipment and radars in the Griffins to find the faults ASAP and to correct them even faster.

Red, of course, took this order in his usual calm, quiet, objective manner. His initial response could be heard all over the small airfield.

A few minutes later, he sent a mechanic racing to track down Wolff and Mugabe where they were waiting in the makeshift pilot's ready room for their next call to action. The man found the two flyers watching a rerun of the old TV show *Blue Thunder* on the big-screen TV in the pilots' lounge at the base of the control tower.

"Wolfman? Mojo?" he said, sticking his head round the corner of the door. "Red wants to see you two guys ASAP."

Wolff looked over at the door. "Tell him we'll be there as soon as this show's over."

The man looked absolutely panic-stricken. "You guys had better come right now," he said. "Red's really pissed off about something."

"What is it this time?"

"I don't know," the mechanic shrugged. "But he just threw the coffeepot out the window."

Wolff got to his feet. "We'd better get going, Mojo. The last time Red did that was when he found that someone had been taking civilians for unauthorized joy rides and letting them play with the sensor controls until they got them all sorts of buggered up."

"But you haven't had enough free time to do something stupid like that," Mojo grinned.

"I know," Wolff said. "So we'd better get over there and find out what's wrong. It's got to be serious this time."

When the two flyers got to the maintenance office, Red was still foaming at the mouth. It didn't help that he had forgotten to fill his coffee cup before he had launched the pot out the window. The caffeine deprivation was doing nothing to improve his mood.

Wolff carefully stepped around the remains of the coffee maker, being very careful not to get any of the brew on his boots—that stuff could ruin a shine forever. "What's up, Chief?" he greeted him.

"What's up? What's up?" Red roared. "I'll tell you what's fucking up! Some limp-dick, candy-ass, paper-shuffling tech weenie back at Denver thinks we haven't been doing the fucking scheduled calibration checks on the Griffin sensors. He's accusing me of allowing them to go down so that you couldn't track those bandits."

The maintenance chief spit out the soggy end of the dead cigar he had bit off and continued his tirade. "And he's ordered me…" He waved a piece of paper in the air. "Ordered me, to deadline all of our birds immediately so they can be inspected."

"So…" Wolff said carefully, eyeing the broken window. Red's temper was legendary, but he had hit a new high this time and the pilot didn't want to get caught in the line of fire if he could help it. "What does that have to do with Mojo and me?"

"What does it have to do with you two assholes?" Red came out of his chair like he had been shot. "I'll tell you exactly what it has to do with you two. This whole thing's your fault. There's not a goddamned thing wrong with those sensors! The only thing that's wrong is that you two hot dogs can't find your ass with both hands and a—"

Mojo walked over to Red and stopped in front of him, his arms held loosely at his side. "I think it's about time that you got hold of yourself, Red," he said quietly.

Red's mouth hung open.

"We all know that you're a real badass," Mugabe continued. "But I think I've had about enough of this today. When you decide to knock off this wild man act, I'll come back and talk to you."

Red's mouth remained open as Mugabe turned and walked out the door. Wolff quickly followed him out onto the tarmac before Red recovered.

"What the hell's wrong with you, man?" he asked. "Are you tired of living? Red's eaten guys alive for a whole lot less than that."

Mugabe stopped outside the hangar door and leaned back against the door frame. "Haven't you figured out yet that Red's all hot air? It's nothing but a bullshit act," he said. "As soon as he calms down we'll go back in there and find out what in the hell's going on."

"I sure as hell hope you know what you're doing," Wolff said. "I don't need Red on my case right now. I've got enough to worry about."

"Trust me."

A few minutes later, Red stepped out of his office. "Hey, Mojo, Wolfman!" he called out. "Can you come in here for a minute, please?"

Wolff turned to Mojo with a look of amazement on his face. "Did I hear him say please?"

"What'd I tell you," Mugabe grinned. "Now we can find out what he's got his shorts in a knot about this time."

"I just got this in," Red said, handing the inspection order to Mugabe. "It's about why you guys couldn't pick up those Mangustas in the air."

Mugabe quickly read through the attached intelligence analysis of the reports. "I'll be a son of a bitch," he said softly. "Those bastards are doing something to jam our sensors."

Wolff looked over his co-pilot's shoulder to read the report, too. "But I thought our stuff was state-of-the-art gear and all that," he said. "Unbeatable and unjammable."

"It was," Mugabe corrected him. "But you've got to remember that the Griffins were designed several years ago and science marches on."

"Is there anything we can do to counter this, Red?" Wolff asked.

The maintenance chief shook his head. "Damned if I know," he said. "Like Mojo said, the electronics packages in the Griffin are several years old now. I know that the military's got better stuff right now than we do, but till now, it hasn't made any real difference to us. The guys we've been coming up against haven't even had gear as good as ours. But if these guys are flying stealth choppers, then we've got us a real problem."

"But I don't understand," Wolff said. "I thought there was no way in hell that you could hide the radar signature of a spinning rotor blade—"

"They used to think the earth was flat, too," Mojo broke in. "Obviously, someone's figured out a way to do it. And, if they're that far advanced it means that they've really got us outclassed. We're blind to them, but I'll bet that they're sure as shit able to see us coming."

"No wonder we couldn't find those bastards yesterday," Wolff said. "We might as well have been chasing them in a hot-air balloon."

"We've got to tell Buzz about this," Mugabe said. "He needs to pass this on to Washington ASAP. We may have to cancel both of these operations till we can get our sensors and radars upgraded."

"With what?" Red sounded bleak. "We've got the best police equipment in the world."

"Then we'd better find out where those maggots bought their stuff and go buy us some, too."

"That's the problem," Red said. "Finding out where they got it."

Buzz was not at all happy to see the three men come into

his office. Neither one of the two current operations was going very well, and this visit could only mean that there was some new problem that had to be dealt with.

"What is it now?" he asked wearily.

"We've got us a problem, sir," Red said.

That got Buzz's complete attention. Red only called him sir when there was something terribly wrong.

"We figured out what's gone wrong every time we've encountered those Mangustas," the maintenance chief continued. "they're stealth choppers."

"Bullshit!" Buzz exploded. "You can't hide a fucking chopper from radar."

"They're not hiding it, sir." Red explained. "But they are blocking our sensors and our targeting radars somehow."

Buzz closed his eyes for a brief moment. This was all he needed right now. "Tell me about it."

Red launched into a long technical explanation of what had happened and how he thought the Mangustas were doing it. He didn't spare the technical details, either. Buzz was not only a pilot, he had a good understanding of electronics as well, particularly Griffin electronics.

"And," Red concluded, "I don't know anything we can do to counter this other than fitting all new equipment."

When Red was finished, Buzz looked out the window for a moment. He knew there had been a good reason that he hadn't wanted this assignment. He had never had much luck in California. In fact, his first wife had been from LA, a fact he tried to forget.

"I'd better get on the horn to Washington with this right away," he said. "Some of the other federal agencies use our type of sensors in their choppers, too, and they'll need to get the word out ASAP."

"I'd tell 'em to keep this classified as much as they can, too, sir," Red suggested. "For them to have done this, someone had to have given them the specs on our black boxes. Someone who knows our gear inside and out."

"You're saying that someone in the Tac Force compromised our equipment?"

"Yes, sir," Red nodded. "There's no other way they could have done this. Those jammers have to operate specifically on our frequencies, specifically our C band radar frequency. If it was a random or a seek-and-lock-type jammer, we'd pick it up on our ECM threat sensors. As it is, it only affects our equipment without showing up anywhere else, so it was specifically tailored to work against Griffins."

Buzz was thoughtful for a moment. "I'll be damned," he said softly. "That means we've got us a bad chopper cop."

"Yes, sir, I'm afraid that it does."

Buzz reached for the phone on his desktop. "Ruby," he said. "Put me through to Internal Affairs in Washington. And, Ruby, put it on the scrambler, please." When Buzz finished making his report he put the phone back down. "For now," he told the men, "this doesn't go out of this room. Until further notice, this information is on a strict need-to-know basis. Until Internal Affairs can locate whoever is responsible for this, we've got to keep it to ourselves."

"But it couldn't be anyone from our Dragon Flight who did it," Wolff said. "We're the ones who stumbled into this."

"Exactly," Buzz said. "You stumbled into it, like you say. But those Mangustas are only operating in our territory. They were set up so they could counter us, specifically us, because we're the only police force who could be affected by their jamming."

Understanding swept over Wolff's face. "I'll be damned," he said softly. "We've been suckered."

CHAPTER 14

Downtown Los Angeles

Sandra felt more than a little silly as she walked down the street at Gunner's side. The short skirt, fish-net stockings, and see-through blouse she was wearing made her feel like she was marching in a parade for perverts. They had been on the street for a little more than an hour and already she was starting to rethink her bright idea about going undercover to try to clear herself.

Unlike most of the male officers in Dragon Flight, she had not done any cop time on the streets before joining the chopper cops. She had been a flyer first, a cop second, and she hadn't fully realized what it was like to walk the late-night streets of urban America. The streets of LA weren't as bad yet as most of those in New York. It wasn't a combat zone with a nightly body count in the dozens, but it wasn't a stroll through the park, either.

Walking through downtown LA at night was almost like walking through the war-torn ruins of Beirut or Baghdad. The tall buildings weren't blasted rubble, but the streets were filled with trash and debris. What had once been a crowded island of multimillion-dollar concrete-and-glass monuments to capitalism was now a derelict jungle of cracked concrete and broken glass. The sightless eyes of shattered windows gazed out onto the dimly lit streets below. Security doors had been battered off of their hinges and stood gaping open. A thick stench of urine, feces, and unwashed bodies mixed with the smell of small fires cooking drugs filled her nostrils. The once-proud bastions of the affluent were now the rat warrens of the drug-craved.

Downtown LA was no longer the home of the American Dream, unless that dream was drug-induced.

They had been on the street for over an hour, but they were no closer to finding what they wanted than they had been before they had arrived. If this had been a real undercover police operation, they would have had some concrete information to start out with, but as it was, they were flying completely blind.

Gunner had convinced her that he would be able to ferret out some kind of lead before too long, but now that they were actually hitting the bricks, she wasn't all that sure that they would find out anything they could use. More and more, this was looking like the premier dumb shit idea of the new decade, if not the new century.

There was no shortage of drug dealers in the abandoned, concrete canyons of downtown LA. The shadowy figures of men and boys hiding in the ruined buildings every few yards called out as they passed, offering everything from grass to 'edge'. It was a drug supermarket. She also noticed that about one in five of the dealers was selling 'edge', and they all mentioned low, low prices.

As with all too many businesses, even in the year 2000, however, there were few women in the LA drug trade. The only women she saw were burned-out addicts, hooking to try to pay for their next "do." Seeing Sandra with Gunner, they didn't bother trying to solicit business from him. They knew that they couldn't compete with the tall good-looking blonde and casually wondered what she was doing slumming in the gutter with them. She should have been turning her tricks in an expensive condo apartment.

Sandra was definitely not the clinging type, but she unconsciously kept close to Gunner's side as they slowly made their way down the dark sidewalks. Even so, only the comforting hardness of her Beretta 6.35mm against the inside of her left thigh gave her any feeling of real protection.

Before they left the motel, they had decided that it would be too dangerous for both of them to go out armed. Even though most of the dealers were armed to the teeth, there would be less tension if Gunner was clean when he tried to make a contact. She, however, was not about to step outside without her back-up piece and had insisted on taking her Beretta with her. That was why she was wearing the short skirt that made her feel so ridiculous; it gave her instant access to the little pistol.

After talking briefly to a couple of the 'edge' salesmen, Gunner decided to wait and watch the action for a while to see if he could spot their sales manager. He found a seat in the shadows on a window ledge of what had once been a bank building where they could watch most of the block. Sandra sat huddled beside the pilot and watched the various transactions taking place in the dim light.

Cars would drive by, circle the block, slow down, and finally stop. A figure would appear from the shadows and lean over an open car window for a moment. After a hurried conversation, the figure would fade back into the darkness and the car would drive on. Sometimes, one of the women would get into the car and drive off; minutes later she would be back. Even though the police had almost abandoned this area, the dealers and whores acted as if they were under surveillance and in imminent danger of being busted and hauled away in the paddy wagon. Old habits die hard.

Sandra shivered, but not from the cold. This wasn't a life for humans. At best, it was mere existence, and a meaningless one at that.

After they had been watching for well over an hour,

Gunner noticed a black man going around to the 'edge' dealers, talking to each of them briefly before moving on. He had to be the midlevel distributor and the man who could put them on the right track to the supplier.

Gunner stepped out of the shadows. "Yo!" he called out. "Hey, bro!"

The man spun around, the muzzle of a 9mm Uzi submachine gun poking out from under his open nylon windbreaker. Gunner held his hands out, his palms forward. "Hey, man, chill out. I'm not packin'. Can we talk?"

Sandra stood off to Gunner's side, her feet spread a foot apart and her hips cocked to one side. She was ready to go for the Beretta but knew that she would be too late if the guy decided to fire.

"You wanna buy something, man?"

Gunner shook his head. "No, man, I just want to rap."

"'Bout what?" The dealer frowned. The muzzle of the Uzi didn't waver an inch.

Gunner grinned. "Well, I'd kinda like to go into business, you know what I mean? And I was thinking that maybe you could give me a hand."

"Why would I wanna do that?"

"I was thinkin' that I could give you a cut, man," Gunner replied. "You know, kinda like a sales commission for helping me to get started."

The man was silent for a moment; then he laughed. "Yeah, man, a commission." The dealer's eyes flicked over to Sandra and she stiffened. He looked back at Gunner.

"What's your name?" he asked.

"They call me Gunner."

"Where do they call you that?"

"I just did a nickel at the Reagan federal slam."

"What ya do to get five years with the feds?"

"Them fuckin' chopper cops busted me for running an air

service, you know?"

"Like into Mexico, you mean?"

"Yeah," Gunner replied. "Mexico and points south. They caught me trying to come back one night and I couldn't get rid of the stuff in time."

The drug dealer chuckled. "Yeah, man, them motherfuckers will do that to ya. That's some bad-ass heat. So, you wanting to get back into the pipeline business?"

"No." Gunner shook his head. "They took away my license so I can't fly no more. I want to get something going on the streets. Maybe get a dealership, you know?"

"Look," the dealer said. "You come back here tomorrow night and I might have something for ya. I gotta talk to my main man first."

"Sure," Gunner grinned. "What's your name?"

The Uzi's muzzle lined up on Gunner again. "You don't worry 'bout that, man," the dealer said. "And you don't be asking nobody about me, either, you hear? You just be here tomorrow, man. I'll find you."

"Sure, man," Gunner said. "Sure."

As soon as the dealer walked around the corner, Sandra relaxed. "Can we go now?" she asked.

Sandra sat at the booth in the coffee shop, her hands cradled around the cup of weak but hot brew. Now that they had actually made contact with a drug dealer, she was sure that she had made a serious mistake. Staring at the muzzle of the Uzi for what had seemed like hours had turned her idea into something far more serious than a mere quest for information. That guy would have gunned them down with just the slightest provocation.

Gunner came back with two plates and laid a hot Danish in front of her.

"Thanks." She wasn't hungry, but she knew that she needed to eat and cut a piece of the pastry. It was as tasteless as the coffee, but it was loaded with sugar and would do until she really felt like eating. She was still so wired on adrenaline that she was almost shaking as she cut another bite.

"Gunner."

"Yeah."

"Maybe this isn't such a good idea after all." She looked down at her cup. "That guy was an inch away from killing you and there was no way that I could have gotten to my piece in time to stop him."

Gunner nodded and took another sip of his coffee. "Yeah," he said slowly. "Those guys are professionally paranoid and he obviously thought that we were cops."

She looked up at him. "And we *are* cops."

"We were, you mean," he corrected her. "Right now, we're just citizens and we're every bit as likely to be on the make as any other citizen."

"Gunner?"

"Yeah."

"Is it really that easy for you?" she asked. "I mean you've been a cop far longer than I have."

"What do you mean?"

"Giving up your badge that way. Becoming a citizen, as you put it."

Gunner took a sip of his coffee. "I really don't think about it all that much," he lied. "I'm too busy trying to figure out how to get something going on the street."

"Do you really think we'll be able to find out anything that I can use?"

He shagged. "I don't know, but it's better than sitting around waiting for the ax to fall."

She took another bite of the pastry. "I sure hope so."

CHAPTER 15

Torrance Airfield, Los Angeles

Morning at Dragon Flight's temporary home did not dawn bright and sunny. For one thing, the offshore breeze had stopped during the night and an inversion layer had formed over the city trapping the smog and dimming the sun. And, to add to the dismal weather, both of the Griffins were grounded until someone could figure out what to do about countering the stealth choppers. The two Griffins working on the border were still flying because it was primarily a daytime mission and they could eyeball the aerial traffic they were tracking instead of having to rely on their sensors and radar. Also, the renegade Mangustas had not been spotted in their operational area yet, so they would keep flying until they were.

The stealth chopper problem, however, was receiving the highest priority from the Tac Force and by noon a team of civilian electronic techs flew in from Bell with completely new radar and sensor packages for the Griffins. Bell had had them in development for the Stage II Griffin that was undergoing testing, so they were compatible with the rest of the chopper's systems and would bolt right in.

As Mojo had accurately stated, the Griffins were not state of the art anymore and they grew more and more obsolete with each passing day. Time and technology did not stand still too anyone, not even the chopper cops. Bell Helicopter had known this all along, of course, which is why they had been working on updating their ship. Their remaining in business depended on their having the best equipment that money could buy and they didn't want to hear that someone had been able to render their once-powerful Griffin impotent. That's why they were on the scene, to put teeth and talons back into their machines.

While the Griffins were being worked on, Wolff and Mugabe were completely at loose ends. They tried their best to help Red in any way that they could, but installing the new electronics packages was a little more than either one of them could handle. In fact, all they were doing was getting in the road of the trained technicians.

By midafternoon, Red finally called them off to one side. "Look, boys," he said. "I really appreciate your help, but why don't you two take the rest of the day off. Go out on the town or something and see if you can scare up some action, you know." He winked. "Check out the local talent. Who knows, maybe you'll get lucky."

"That's not a bad idea," Wolff said, wiping his hands on a grease rag. "What'd you say, Mojo? You want to go cruise a few dives tonight?"

The black gunner was well aware that Red was just trying to get rid of them, but it had been a long time since they'd had a chance to kick back and relax. It would probably do both of them some good to get out on the town. "Sure," he said. "Let's do it."

After getting cleaned up and changing into their civilian clothes, the two flyers got a couple of hot tips from the LAPD officers about the local establishments where an off-duty cop would be welcomed instead of getting mugged in the men's room. They also managed to talk one of the guys out of the use of his car for the evening. Usually, Mojo managed to ship his big Kawasaki bike in with the cargo loads when Dragon Flight displaced to a temporary base. But, since only part of the support team had flown in this time, there had been no room for the bike on the single C-9 cargo plane that had brought the team to LA.

The first place they stopped was the local cop hangout for the off-duty officers from the airfield. Like all cop hangouts, it resembled a police briefing room more than it did a tavern. Holos of police officers covered the walls interspaced with plaques, mounting badges, and patches from other police departments. Shelves of dusty shooting trophies ran the entire perimeter of the room.

The bartender gave Mojo a close look when they sat down. Not too many cops had their heads shaved or wore a gold earring in one ear. Wolff's longish blond locks and leather flight jacket got a glance, too, but since they both looked so much at home, she figured them for undercover guys and took their order. "What'll ya have?"

"A couple of drafts."

As they sat nursing their beers, they looked around the bar. It was easy to spot the off-duty cops; they all had short haircuts and black shoes. It was even easier to spot the local police groupies. They all had a faintly frantic look about them as if this was their last chance to latch on to a steady paycheck.

"It's too bad Gunner and Legs aren't here tonight," Mugabe said.

"Speaking of Gunner and Legs," Wolff said. "I want to try to get a hold of them tomorrow. I don't want them to think that they've been completely forgotten."

In the rush of the last three days, Legs and Gunner had almost been forgotten about except for the fact that their absence from Dragon Flight was what was causing them to be forgotten. With Wolff and Mugabe being on call twenty-four hours a day, there had been no way for the two fliers to get away to check in on them. Since Red was going to be working on the choppers for at least another day, however, it shouldn't be a problem for them to get away for a couple of hours in the morning.

"You want to stop by tonight and see if they want to go out for a beer?"

Wolff shook his head as he looked around the room. "Na, let's catch them in the morning for breakfast. I want to see what LA has to offer."

He finished his beer with a gulp. "Let's book," he said. "Nothing's happening here. This is just another damned cop shop and I've had it with cops for the last couple of days."

"Where you want to go?"

"Someplace where I don't have to look at police badges," he answered, glancing up at the wall.

Mojo laughed.

The next place they stopped wasn't all that much better than the cop hangout, but at least the women were. They were less frantic, but still hungry, which suited Wolff just fine as he slid into a chair at a table against one wall and waved for the waitress.

When their beers came, Wolff quickly scanned the women in the crowd, scouting for interesting prospects. There were several likely candidates, but his eyes kept going back to a stunning blonde sitting at a table with her girlfriend, a passable brunette with spectacular breasts.

"What'd you think?" he asked Mojo.

Mugabe glanced over at the table. "Which one?"

"The blonde."

Mojo shrugged. "Give it a shot, it can't hurt. You know what they say, 'Faint heart never won fair hand.'"

"Who said that?"

"Damned if I know."

Wolff called the waitress over again and told her to give the blond girl a drink on his tab. The waitress looked slightly disgusted with him as if that sort of thing was just not done in her establishment but went to get the drink anyway. She took a giant pink margarita over to the girl and, leaning down to whisper in her ear, handed her the glass.

Wolff watched with his best, most fetching smile on his face as the girl took the margarita. She looked over at him, poured it out on the floor, and shot him the finger.

Mojo collapsed in laughter.

"Screw it," Wolff said, ignoring his partner. "Let's go get something to eat."

"Suits me."

Legs and Gunner were back in the concrete canyons of downtown LA by ten o'clock that night for their appointment with the dealer.

Sandra's costume was even more outrageous than it had been the night before, but Gunner had pointed out that it would be a good idea if she showed a little more skin. If for no other reason, it might be a good diversion if things got out of hand tonight. No heterosexual male, however well trained, could keep from glancing over at bare female flesh. It was just the way evolution had wired the male brain. Legs's going into action would draw any man's attention and might keep Gunner from getting killed if shots were exchanged.

Even though she knew what she was going into this time, Sandra was still shocked when she walked back into the shadows of the crumpling, abandoned skyscrapers, and the overwhelming stench that permeated everything hit her again. Downtown LA was so contaminated that all it was good for was a site for a future nuclear waste dump. This time, they didn't bother to cruise the street, but just reclaimed their seats in the bank building's windowsill and sat down to wait for their contact.

Two hours later, as midnight drew closer, they were about to give up and go back to the motel. Suddenly, the dealer appeared. Gunner stepped out into the open to greet him. "Yo, bro! Over here."

The dealer turned around. The muzzle of his Uzi was poking out from under his jacket again but not in a threatening manner. Sandra, however, didn't relax for an instant. Again, she stood well off to Gunner's side, ready to make a grab for her pistol if the meeting went bad.

"You got somethin' for me," Gunner asked.

"Yeah, man," the dealer said, glancing over to Legs. "But you gotta leave your lady here. I don't like getting a lot of people involved in my business, you know."

"No way, man," Gunner shook his head. "She goes everywhere I go. I don't ever let that woman outta my sight for a minute."

The dealer laughed, looking back at Legs. "You a lot smarter than you look, man. You leave that stuff on the street and you won't have her very long, that's a fact."

"You got that shit right."

The dealer relented. "Okay," he said. "Come on, I've got my ride around the corner."

"Where we going?" Gunner asked.

"We going to meet my main man," the dealer said. "He's the one who can help you get set up."

The dealer's ride was a red '92 Cadillac, the last year that GM had made the huge, gas-guzzling, land barges. Caddies weren't even manufactured anymore. General Motors had dropped all three of their big car lines in '98 when the mandatory downsizing turned them into little more than overpriced, poorly built compact cars unable to compete with the Japanese and Korean designs.

Like the dinosaurs they resembled, Caddies were ancient history in the year 2000, but they were still popular with the criminal element. And the bigger, the better.

Playing the role as a hood, Gunner stepped into the front passenger seat of the Caddy without even helping Sandra open the rear door. As a drug dealer's bimbo, she would be expected to do those little things for herself.

Wolff and Mugabe were completely lost and they were rounding the corner onto the broad boulevard running down through the downtown business district when they spotted the tall blonde stepping into the backseat of the fire-engine-red Caddy.

"Hey," Wolff said. "Isn't that Legs over there?"

Mugabe looked closer and saw the miniskirt, the see-through blouse, and the fishnet stockings. "No fucking way," he laughed. "Legs wouldn't be caught dead wearing something like that."

"Yeah, I guess you're right," Wolff said, peering up to try to read the street signs try the dim light. "What in the hell are we supposed to be looking for?"

"A place to eat."

CHAPTER 16

The Raging Surf Motel, Los Angeles

There was little conversation on the drive to meet the drug supplier. The dealer didn't offer anything and Gunner knew better than to try to pump him for information. This was not the time for that and, now that they were on their way, he hoped he'd find out what he wanted to know soon enough. Sandra sat in the back and did not say a word. She didn't want to say anything that might kill the deal, and until Gunner developed a lead, she was truly just along for the ride. She did, however, keep her right hand in her lap next to the butt of the little Beretta pistol.

Their destination turned out to be a run-down, 1970's California kitsch motel hiding around the corner from what had once been a public beach park. Now it was a drug shooting gallery that smelled like a public toilet and looked like an unkempt annex to the city dump. A dead palm tree was on fire from top to bottom, serving to illuminate the festivities. Sandra saw the blackened stumps of the other trees that had once encircled the little park and wondered what the drug maggots would do when the last tree had been burned—start burning the buildings across the street?

The dealer turned his Caddy into the motel parking lot and braked to a stop in front of number 12, the last room on the first floor.

The rest of the parking lot was deserted except for a van on resting blocks by the office. "Real nice place," Sandra whispered, trying to break the tension. "I wonder if they take reservations."

Gunner grunted, but didn't answer. He was confident that he could handle anything that came up tonight, but there was still the pucker factor to deal with. These guys were less than stable and there was always the chance that something could go tits up. He would have felt much more comfortable if they had a backup of some kind—maybe one of the Tac teams hiding around the corner or a Griffin on station.

The dealer knocked on the door and, when a man's voice inside told them to come in, he held the door open so Gunner and Sandra could enter first.

In the faint light from the lamp on the night table, Gunner saw a man standing by the side of the room's narrow bed holding a .357 Magnum in his hand. Behind him, a teenage girl sat on the rumpled bed, apparently oblivious to anything that was going on around her.

Gunner tensed at the sight of the gun, but as soon as the supplier saw Legs and the dealer, he relaxed and laid the pistol on the nightstand, but still within quick reach.

"Come on in," the man said, gesturing toward the two worn easy chairs against the wall on the other side of the room. "Have a seat."

Gunner and Legs sat, but the street dealer stood, leaning against the wall behind them, his hand on the pistol grip of the Uzi. They were in a bad tactical position with one gun in front of them and another one behind, but Gunner tried to relax anyway. Body language meant a great deal in this kind of negotiation.

"My man here," the supplier said, nodding to the dealer, "says that you're thinking of going into business for yourself."

Gunner grinned. "Well, you know, man, a guy's gotta

make his payments and keep the ladies happy."

The supplier had a slight trace of an accent and, to Gunner's ears, it sounded East Coast, but he wasn't sure. The man was definitely dressed in East Coast fashion, however. No one west of the Rockies would wear a black body shirt open to the navel and red bellbottom pants. His dark, slicked-back hair also marked him as being from the East Coast, either that or south of the border.

Gunner immediately tagged him "Slick."

The girl on the bed, however, was pure California; a golden tan setting off long golden blond hair and deep-blue eyes, skintight cut-off blue jeans and a bulging halter top. He could see that she would have been pretty if she were cleaned up and had her hair combed. He could also see that she would become stunningly beautiful if she were ever to reach her full maturity. But, from the angry red needle tracks on both her arms, the vacant look in her darkly shadowed eyes, and the slack, garishly painted mouth, he knew that wasn't very likely. The way she was going, she'd be lucky to live out the year. Even lasting to the end of the month was going to be real iffy for this chick.

There were thousands of teenage girls like her in LA, or in any other big American city for that matter. Girls who were more than willing to exchange sex and a life of degradation for an endless supply of free drugs and an early grave. If she didn't die of an overdose first, her boyfriend would simply toss her young ass out on the street as soon as he got bored with her and wanted to screw someone who wasn't half dead.

"He also says," Slick continued, "that you got yourself busted for running shit in from south of the border. Tell me about that."

"You know," Gunner shrugged, "I was a chopper pilot doing an aerial taxi number and I had a pretty good little pipeline going on the side for a while. I was freelancing, you know, mostly blow. But, I was moving anything I could get my hands on before I got nailed by the fuckin' chopper cops."

"How'd that happen?"

Gunner grinned and gave Slick the story of one of his own aerial drug busts on the Mexican border, but with the roles reversed.

"It was a moonless night and I was coming in fast and low," he said. "'Bout twenty miles east of T Town. I had my radar detector going and it looked clear. Suddenly, I had two of those motherfuckers right on top of me. They came outta nowhere, switched their searchlights on, and there was nothing I could do, you know. I didn't have anyone in the back, so I couldn't dump the stuff. They forced me down and found five keys of black tar."

As Gunner talked, Slick made notes in a little book. "And then what happened?"

Gunner shrugged. "The usual, I copped a plea and did five in Reagan."

"When'd you get out?"

"A couple of months ago."

"What've you been doing since then?"

"This and that," Gunner shrugged. "A buddy of mine had this little chop shop going and I was giving him a hand with it. But, that's not my action, you know. There's just not enough in it to make it worthwhile. I'm looking for something that's got a little more in it for me."

"You thinkin' 'bout 'edge'?"

Gunner grinned widely. "That'd be fine, man, real fine. I understand that shit's doing real good now."

"You a user?"

Gunner looked offended. "No fuckin' way, man. I never touch any of that shit. I know better than that, man. I'm a juicer."

"Okay, man," the supplier said. "I'll tell you what. I'll pass this on and try to get you an interview with some people who might be able to help you. I can't guarantee nothin', you know, but I'll put you in touch with them. Where're you staying now?"

Gunner gave him the address of their motel, his room number and phone number.

"You make sure you're there tomorrow morning about eight thirty, nine o'clock," he said. "And I'll send someone around to pick you up."

"I'll be there," Gunner promised.

Slick closed his notebook and glanced over at Legs. "Now that we've got the business out of the way, what you say we party?"

He nodded toward his girlfriend before looking back to Legs. "Sweet thing over there gives real good head. And since we're going to be in business together, maybe we should get a little better acquainted, you know. I've got some good shit for the ladies, really get 'em going"

Sandra stiffened, her hands edging for the pistol, but Gunner laid his hand on her and grinned. "I'd really like to, man," he said. "But my lady's still getting her shots, so we'd better not tonight."

Slick looked real disappointed, but he knew better than to risk it. Some of the stuff that was going around now was serious and he wasn't about to take the chance of ruining his love life for a little strange stuff. It was too bad; the tall blonde didn't look like she was stupid enough to have gotten herself dosed up. It only went to show that you could never trust first impressions.

"Yeah," the supplier said, taking a last look at Legs. "Maybe another time."

Sandra relaxed.

The dealer dropped Gunner and Legs off outside their motel and, as soon as he was out of sight, the two cops walked over to the coffee shop across the street. Both of them were too keyed up to sleep and they wanted to talk about the "job interview" with the supplier. They both got coffee and took a booth well away from the other late-night customers.

"Jesus," Sandra said softly. "When I saw that guy standing there with a gun in his hand, I thought we'd walked into a setup for sure."

"Not really," Gunner replied. "That's just the way those guys work. Like I said, they're professionally paranoid. It goes with the job."

"You think we're finally on to something?"

Gunner was silent for a moment. "Yeah, but I'm not sure exactly what. I've never heard of drug dealers giving job interviews before."

"Maybe they've got a couple of MBA's running the organization," Sandra smiled. "Equal opportunity employment, résumés and all that."

"Right. What was it that they used to call the Wall Street hustlers? Yuppies?"

"I thought it was Muppies."

"Maybe they've got Muppies running the show," Gunner grinned. "But whatever it is, I've got to make sure that my cover story holds up."

"How are you going to do that?"

"That story about being in Reagan Federal Prison I gave him? Well, one of my cousins, the black sheep of the family, actually did time in there for a drug bust. He got iced before he got out, but his last name was the same. I'll just use his initials."

"I hope it works."

"So do I," Gunner agreed, looking out the window. "But it should hold up."

After shooting the bolt on the motel door behind her, Sandra walked over to the bed and sat down to unstrap the holster from the inside of her thigh. The damned thing chafed her skin, but she wasn't about to take a step outside the door without it.

Her drug bimbo-hooker's costume quickly followed. Shaking her long hair out of the elaborate hairdo, she stepped into the shower. After just a few hours on the streets of LA, she felt dirty all over.

After a long shower, she dried her hair and lay down on the bed. She was bone-weary, but she didn't go to sleep right away. She had been running on pure adrenaline for the last several hours and her mind was racing. Now that they were on the track to this gang at last, she was starting to lose her confidence. Her plan had made good sense to her a couple of days ago, but now she wasn't so sure.

Gunner still was confident that it would work, however, so she would go with his instincts for now. He knew more about the streets than she did and, since this was her last chance to vindicate herself, she really had no choice but to follow his lead.

CHAPTER 17

The Golden Sunset Motel, Los Angeles

Wolff and Mugabe arrived at Gunner and Legs's motel right after nine the next morning planning that they'd all go out for breakfast together. When no one answered the knock on either of their doors, they went back down to the motel office to see if the clerk knew where they had gone.

"I ain't seen 'em since last night," the clerk said. "They left together at about nine or so and I didn't see 'em come back." The clerk paused. "But then, I get off at midnight, so maybe they came in late." He shrugged. "I don't know."

"What was the woman wearing when they went out?" Mojo asked, working on a hunch.

The clerk smiled. "She was dressed like a hooker on payday night, you know what I mean? Short skirt, high heels, and one of those blouses that you can see right through. And man, did she have something to see, too."

The two cops looked at each other. It had been Legs they had seen downtown last night. "Did you see them get into a red Caddy?"

The clerk shook his head. "No, they stopped a cab out front."

"How about letting us into their rooms," Wolff said. "We

were supposed to meet them here this morning and I want to see if they left us a note or something."

"I can't let you into those rooms." The clerk shook his head. "They didn't tell me anything about meeting friends here. Also, I don't know who you guys are."

Wolff reached into his back pocket and pulled out his identification folder and whipped out his badge. "We're federal cops," he said. "And those two are cops, too."

"I didn't know that they were cops," The clerk looked nervous as he eyed the gold TPF badge. "I'd have kept a closer eye on them if I'd known that."

I'll just bet you would have, Wolff thought. "You weren't supposed to know they were cops," he told the man. "So just get me the key, okay?"

"But aren't you supposed to have a warrant or something first?"

"I can get a warrant," Wolff grinned as he leaned over the counter. "But if I do, I'm also going to get a vice squad-team and have them go over this rattrap one fucking inch at a time."

The clerk immediately reached for the master key. "No need to go to all that trouble, Officer," he said, with a sick-looking smile. "You two just help yourselves. Please bring the key back when you're done."

"Thanks."

"No problem, Officer."

"I wonder what he's got going on the side here?" Mojo asked when they walked out of the office.

Wolff shrugged. "Probably just the usual—a little drugs, a few hookers, who knows."

"I thought prostitution was legal in California."

"That was two years ago," Wolff replied. "The state made it a crime again last year."

Mugabe shook his head. As far as he was concerned, with all the problems facing American society in the new century, commercial sex was the last thing that cops should be wasting their time on. But it seemed that the worse things got, the more local governments wasted their resources on "sin crimes" like sex and gambling. It was almost as if since they couldn't make any real headway against serious crimes, they could always proudly say that they didn't have any adult bookstores or hookers in their towns. He was glad that he was a federal cop so he didn't have to waste his time on silly shit like that.

Wolff and Mojo quickly searched Gunner's and Legs's rooms, but found nothing to indicate where they might have gone. In fact, it was hard to tell what, if anything, was missing from their meager belongings. Both of them had brought very little with them from Denver, just the usual small bag of personal gear that each chopper cop always took on an away-from-home assignment.

"I don't like this," Wolff said. "Other than maybe a change of clothes, everything seems to be here."

Mugabe repacked Gunmen's flight bag and put it back by the bed. "I don't like this either," he agreed. "I knew we should have contacted them earlier."

"We were on duty," Wolff reminded him. "There was no way we could have gotten the time off to come out here."

"Buzz should have sent someone out here to check on them."

"They're both adults," Wolff pointed out. "And they're not chopper cops anymore."

"Goddamnit," Wolff," Mugabe said. "That's not the point. They're still our friends and we left them out here on their own."

"Let's get back and have a little chat with Buzz and get him to put out an APB or them."

Gunner tried to keep track of the route that the driver was

taking, but after the first couple of miles through the outlying districts of greater LA, he was completely turned around and had lost all sense of direction. Looking for the sun was a fruitless exercise in the smog, so he didn't even have that to use as a navigational aid.

Sandra said little on the trip and sat at the opposite side of the car as far away from him as she could get so her gun hand would be free if she had to go for it. She still wasn't comfortable with this and wanted to be ready for anything that happened. The worst thing about this whole idea was that she had become entirely dependent on Gunner and had to follow his lead. Drug dealers' girlfriends couldn't be too pushy.

The trip ended at a business center close to a small airfield. A guard at the gate checked the car before letting it pass through. The driver continued up to a fenced warehouse at the end of the complex.

Gunner's trained eye noticed the extent of the security at the warehouse. It was as professional as the security at the Dragon Flight home base in Denver and included motion sensors, IR seekers, razor wire, remote-control cameras, and what looked to be remote-controlled stun gas grenade launchers. Whoever was behind this operation definitely didn't want anyone snooping in on their business.

A small sign by the warehouse door read Frienzia Pharmaceutical, but Gunner paid no attention to the sign. Obviously it was a dodge; he had read about Frienzia and knew that it was a legit company, a big multinational corporation. The car stopped under the cover of a surveillance camera.

"There it is," the driver turned around to tell him. "Just go in that door and someone will be waiting for ya."

Gunner opened the door and stepped out with Sandra right behind him, "Thanks."

The driver didn't answer.

The door opened and the two of them walked through it

to find themselves in a small anteroom. Two men who had "hood" written all over them were waiting for them. This time, however, the pistols were still in their holsters instead of in their hands.

"Your lady can wait in here," the taller man said, opening a door to a waiting room.

Sandra looked at Gunner, but he shook his head. "Do as the man says. It'll be okay."

As soon as Sandra went into the room, the hoods led Gunner on down the hall to a brightly lit office. The man behind the desk looked like a bit actor in the old *Godfather* movies: slicked-back hair, black shirt, white tic, thin mustache, and thick cigar.

"You're Gunner right?"

"Right."

"And you want to become a part of our family?"

"I'd like to do business with you."

The mafioso looked at him for a long time. "We need to get better acquainted first," he said without smiling. "I need to check your references."

"I gave your man at the motel my rap sheet," Gunner said, beginning to worry.

"Yeah, that's what he said. But I need to check you out before we go any further."

The man reached out and turned on the computer on his desk. "What did you say your name was?"

This was the one thing Gunner hadn't counted on, that this drug gang would be hi-tech, computer literate instead of being just another bunch of psychopathic street maggots who couldn't even turn a computer on, much less use one. He realized that he was out of touch, badly out of touch, with life on the street, and it was probably going to cost him big today.

"Jennings," he answered. "Robert D."

"When were you in Reagan?"

Gunner thought fast. "June '95 till last month."

Gunner glanced at his two guards out of the corners of his eyes as the mafioso punched a series of numbers and letters into his computer keyboard. There was no way that he was going to get out of this room if his cover didn't hold up. The name was real, one of his cousins had done time there, but he had also been killed while he was still in the slammer. If this guy was tapping into police records, he'd be okay, but if he could get into the Reagan Federal Prison records, he was truly and thoroughly fucked.

The man looked up from the monitor. "You got a serious problem here, man."

"What's that?" Gunner tried hard to keep his voice neutral as his mind raced.

"The computer says that you're a liar, and computers never lie. You never did no time at Reagan. At least not under the name you just gave me. A Jennings, Robert D., did time there, but you ain't him. Not by a long shot; he's dead."

The man turned back and started punching keys on the keyboard again. "I think I'd better find out just who in the hell you really are, mister. And if you're what I think you are, you can just stick your head between your legs and kiss your sweet ass good-bye."

Gunner thought fast. All he could do now was to go for it, take the big gamble. "Actually," he said slowly. "I used to be a cop, a chopper cop."

The sound of two pistol hammers being cocked was deafening in the silence.

The mafioso turned around in his swivel chair to face Gunner. "You got a lotta balls, man, I'll admit that. But you're dead meat."

"Wait a minute," Gunner talked fast. "I said I used to be a cop. They threw me out on some phony bullshit charge and I want to get back at the bastards. I know how they operate, man, all their inside stuff and I could be real useful to your operation."

"A bad chopper cop..." the man smiled tightly. "That might prove to be interesting. You'd fit right in with another one of our people."

That comment got Gunner's fullest attention. Was the guy saying that they already had a renegade chopper cop on the payroll? If that was true, it was the answer as to why this operation against the Mangustas had been jinxed right from the start.

"What's your real name?"

"Jennings, Daryl T. Flight Sergeant. Badge number 465-5150."

The mafioso turned to the guards. "Get him outta here for a minute, I gotta make a call."

"Come on, you." One of the guards jabbed him in the ribs with the muzzle of his pistol.

Gunner slowly got to his feet, being very careful not to move too fast. "The girl with me," he said. "She doesn't know anything about this."

The mafioso didn't smile. "We'll take care of her, too, you can count on that."

CHAPTER 18

Frienzia Pharmaceutical, California

The waiting room was also covered by a surveillance camera so Sandra was careful not to do anything that would draw unwanted attention to herself. She grabbed a copy of *New People* magazine from the coffee table and pretended to read it while keeping a close eye on her watch at the same time. She hated not knowing what was happening to Gunner.

She looked up from the magazine when the door suddenly opened, and her heart lurched when two men walked into the room. Both of them had pistols trained on her and neither one of them was smiling.

Something had gone wrong, badly wrong.

"On your feet, bitch!" the short one snarled.

She put the magazine down carefully and slowly got to her feet. "Where's Gunner?" she asked.

"I wouldn't worry about him right now," the tall one said. "You've got enough troubles of your own."

"Get movin'!" the short one snapped, motioning with the barrel of his pistol.

The two men guided her down the hallway to the back of the building. With their two pistols covering her, there was no way that she could go for her Beretta without getting gunned down in an instant. And the martial arts training she was so proud of wasn't going to get her out of this one, either. The karate chop and high-kick routine always worked in the made-for-television movies, but this wasn't prime time. She could probably take one of these guys out, true. But the other one was sure to kill her.

She was halted outside a small office at the end of the hall. The short one kept her covered while the tall one opened the door and motioned her inside.

"Check her good," the tall one said once the door was shut behind them. "Make sure she ain't packin' anything."

"Up against the wall," the short one motioned with his pistol. "And put your hands up high."

There was little room to hide a weapon in her skimpy costume, but Sandra stood stock-still, her arms in the air as the short man leaned down and slowly slid his hand up the inside of her thigh.

"Well, lookie here," he smirked as he pulled the little Beretta from the leg holster. "This bitch's got more than snatch up there."

He tossed the pistol over to his partner and ran his hand up between her legs again. "I'd better see what else she's got up there."

Sandra violently twisted away from his probing fingers and shoved him back with both hands.

"Watch it, bitch!" he snapped, bringing his pistol up to her face.

"You found the gun," she snapped. "So keep your hands off me."

"Keep your hands off me," the thug mimicked in a high-pitched voice. The pistol's muzzle was centered on her left eye as his hand came up to cup her full breast. She stared, unflinching as the thug felt her up.

"We oughta pump this bitch real good before we send her

ass south," he suggested.

"You lay a hand on her and you know who will cut your balls off," the tall man said. "He specifically said that he wants this one untouched."

"Fuck!" the short one complained. "He always gets to keep the choice stuff for himself."

"That's why he's the boss and you're an asshole,"

"All we ever get is brain-dead, junkie bitches you have to throw in a shower before you can pork 'em. And even then, you're running a risk of catching something that'll rot your dick off."

"Quit bitchin', man. At least you're getting some leg, brain dead or not."

The fact that she apparently wasn't going to be gang raped on the spot was not much comfort to Sandra. Neither was the fact that she wasn't going to be killed immediately. Being sent south could only mean that they were planning to take her to Mexico and that could be far worse than a quick clean death. She shuddered when she remembered the reports she had read of American women who had been kidnapped and sold to the whorehouses and drug dens in the Mexican border towns.

"Okay, lady..." The tall thug motioned with his pistol as he opened the door to a storage room off the office. "Get your ass in there. And you'd better behave yourself till we get back."

Sandra walked into the small, windowless room, a perfect detention cell. There was a single light bulb hanging from the ceiling, a small table up against one wall, and two metal folding chairs. She took a seat as the door closed behind her and she heard the turn of a key in the lock. Now that she knew what was going to happen to her, she had time to think about Gunner.

She deeply regretted even suggesting her half-assed plan to go "undercover" to try to solve her problem. She should have known better than to try something as stupid as that. Street work wasn't as easy as it always looked in the cop shows on TV. But she had more than merely suggested the plan. She had insisted on doing it, and Gunner had gone through with it for her sake, as she had known that he would.

Poor Gunner, she had used his loyalty for her to try to get her out of the mess she was in and it had only doomed them both. She had knowingly used him and there wasn't a thing she could do to help him now. It was going to be all she could do just to try to help herself get out of this mess.

She sat with her arms wrapped around herself and waited for the sound of the key in the lock again. There was nothing she could do to help herself now, but from what the tall hood had said, they would be taking her down into Mexico before too much longer. Maybe she would get a better chance to escape then.

All she could do now was wait and hope.

Gunner's hands were going numb from the pressure of the handcuffs locked tightly around his wrists. It had been several hours since he had been taken from the warehouse in California and flown by helicopter to this large hangar. He'd been deposited on the floor of the chopper with two armed goons to guard him during the flight, so he hadn't been able to look out of the window. But he thought that he had been taken to Mexico, somewhere fairly close to the border. At least it smelled like Mexico, not California.

At the hangar, his guard had unlocked one of the cuffs just long enough to bring his hands around behind a two-inch water pipe and re-cuff them before leaving him. He could stand or he could crouch on the concrete floor, but he wasn't going anywhere until they released him.

The cavernous hangar was illuminated only by the sunlight coming through a row of dirty windows high along the top of the wall, In the dim light he could see the crouching, shadowy shape of a red Mangusta helicopter. Squatting on its wide-track landing gear, the Italian gunship looked even more menacing on the ground than it did in the air. He had finally found where the damned things were based, but it wasn't going to do him or Sandra any good.

He heard the distant sound of rotors approaching fast. The unseen chopper circled once low over the hangar and put down right outside the closed main doors, its turbines at an idle. Someone tripped the door-opening circuit and the large doors started sliding open. Gunner twisted around the pipe so he could see what was happening, and as soon as the doors had opened wide enough, he saw the other Mangusta sitting outside in the bright sunlight. As soon as the doors opened wide enough to clear the rotors, the gunship taxied inside the hangar and shut down its turbines.

The Mangusta's canopy opened and two men stepped down from the cockpit. Though the doors were quickly closing again, enough light came in that Gunner could clearly see that the two men were dressed in plain khaki flight suits devoid of patches or other insignia. When they pulled their helmets off, he saw that they were blonde with a European cast to their features. Hidden in the shadows as he was, neither of the men saw him as they walked over to the door leading back outside.

He caught snatches of their unguarded, low conversation, but not enough to recognize the language they were speaking. He only knew that it wasn't English or Spanish.

What in the hell was going on here? European pilots flying Italian gunships and robbing banks in California for a drug gang? Whatever was going on, it was a hell of a lot bigger than he had ever imagined. He and Sandra had been completely out of their minds to think that they could investigate this thing on their own. It was his own damned fault for not insisting that they at least let Wolff and Mugabe in on their plans.

He shifted position to try to restore circulation to his

arms, but there was nothing he could do about his hands; the cuffs were too tight. He knew that someone would come to get him before too long. He just hoped that it would be before he lost the use of his hands.

Buzz listened patiently to Wolff and Mugabe's report on what they had found at the motel room. When they were done, he leaned back in his chair. "I can understand your concern," he said. "But we've got us a little problem here."

"What's that?"

"The obvious one, they're not Tac Force anymore and I don't have any jurisdiction over them. They're citizens now and they can do anything they want. If they're not where they're supposed to be, there's really not a hell of a lot that I can do about it."

"Can't you have an APB put out on them?" Mugabe asked hopefully.

"That's a state police matter," Buzz said. "And, as you well know, they have to be missing for at least twenty-four hours first."

"You're forgetting one thing, sir," Wolff pointed out. "Gunner's resigned, true, but Legs is just on a suspension until the trial. She's still a Tac Force officer and she's missing."

Buzz thought for a moment. "Okay," he said. "I'll put out a federal APB on her, but I'll have to report her as violating the conditions of her suspension and that might not help her at her trial."

"Just do it," Wolff said. "I'll testify that I requested it if I have to, but I'd like to know that someone's out there looking for her."

"The replacement crew for One Four has finally arrived," Buzz said. "I want you to take them in hand and get them briefed into the situation ASAP. Red has promised me that the Griffins will be out of the shop this afternoon, so I want to see you two back in the air this evening. Put the new crew on Ramp Alert."

"Yes, sir."

"And, Wolff?"

"Sir?"

"Don't worry, Gunner and Legs will show up."

"Yes, sir."

When Wolff and Mojo left Buzz's office, the pilot stopped at the end of the hall. "You go on and see how Red is coming along with One Zero," he told Mojo.

"What're you going to do?"

"Since we're going out again tonight, I want to try and find us some targets."

"What in the hell are you talking about?"

"Red Caddies," Wolff grinned. "I'm going to get Mom to do a rundown on all the late-model red Caddies in LA."

"What are you going to do when you find them?"

"I thought we'd have a little chat with the drivers about a tall blonde dressed like a hooker."

"Good idea," Mojo smiled broadly. "But make sure that you include all the orange and maroon Caddies too. The light wasn't all that good down there that night. It might not have been red."

"Don't worry," Wolff promised. "I'll get them, every last one of them."

CHAPTER 19

Torrance Airfield, Los Angeles

By the time that Mugabe returned to the flight line, Red was in the process of towing the two Griffins back out onto the tarmac. Mojo walked up to him. "You finished with them?"

Red fished into the breast pocket of his coveralls for a fresh cigar. "Yep." he said proudly. "They're better than ever now. Your new target acquisition radar is G Band, a higher frequency than our old sets, and it's tied in with a new gun-laying system. Now you'll be able to lock your weapons onto one target and still continue to track a second one at the same time."

He took Mojo by the arm. "Come here, I'll show you. I think you'll like what we've done."

Red quickly went over the changes to the weapons controls and radar systems. "See, there's nothing to it," he said when he was finished.

Mojo was impressed. Red had done a good job. The Griffins should have had that "shoot one, track one" capability all along. Now, the next time they encountered the Mangustas, they would be able to get their licks in for a change instead of looking like complete assholes.

But, along with the new radar and fire control, he needed

one more thing, something to shoot.

"Red?"

"Yeah?"

"Did you bring the armament kits with you?"

"I brought the B load kits," Red frowned. "Why?"

"You wouldn't happen to have a 25mm package in there, would you?"

Red transferred his dead cigar butt to the other side of his mouth and rubbed the back of his neck with one hand. "I've got one," he admitted. "But Buzz hasn't said anything to me about mounting the heavy hardware yet."

Mojo's eyes held Red in their gaze. "I don't want to get into a pissing contest with you, Red," he said softly. "But I'd like to have that gun put in my ship. And I'd like to have it mounted most ricky tick."

Red smiled faintly at hearing the old, familiar military slang. "Where'd you learn to say that?"

Mojo didn't smile back. "Gunner's not the only one around here who watches old Vietnam War movies. I'd like the twenty-five put in and I'd like it done right now, before we go out tonight."

Red chewed on the dead cigar butt for a moment. "Well, I guess that since you work with Wolff and since he's the Dragon Flight leader, I can do that for you without checking with Buzz first."

Mugabe looked Red straight in the eyes. "Thanks."

Red smiled. "No sweat, Mojo, we're all in this together, right?"

"Right."

"If you don't mind my asking," Red said, "just what are you boys planning to do with the heavy hardware?"

Mojo thought for a moment and finally decided to trust Red. "Have you heard that Gunner and Legs are missing from their motel?"

"I did hear something about it," he said. "No details, though."

"We don't have any details, either," Mojo said. "We only know they've been missing since last night. So Wolff and I thought that we'd spend a little time looking for them tonight."

"With a 25mm chain gun?"

"There's some bad-assed people on the streets of LA," Mojo smiled tightly. "And you never can tell when you might need a little backup."

Red shook his head. "I sure as hell hope that you two boys know what you're doing."

"So do I."

Sandra stood up when she heard the key turn in the lock. The door opened revealing the tall hood standing well back out of the way as he covered her with his pistol. The short thug stood with a set of plastic restraints ready to slip over her wrists.

"Okay, lady," the tall one said. "Let's get a move on it. Your ride's here."

"Where are you taking me?"

"Don't worry about it," the man grinned. "You're going to love it. You're going to meet an old friend."

"Who?"

"He says he's an old friend of yours from your chopper cop days."

If he knew that she had been a chopper cop, then they knew about Gunner, too. "Where's the guy I came with, Gunner?" she asked.

"I wouldn't worry about him," he answered. "He's rather busy right now."

"Just shut the fuck up and put your arms behind your back," the short one snapped. He was still pissed that Sandra was getting away from him.

She silently did as she was told and he quickly slipped the restraints over her wrists and cinched them down as tightly as he could.

"Okay, let's go," the tall one said, taking her arm.

A small blue-and-white Bell executive helicopter sat outside on the tarmac, its main rotor spinning at an idle. As she got closer to it, she saw that it wore a Frienzia Pharmaceutical badge on the door. She couldn't figure out why the gang was using Frienzia as a cover, but she knew that there had to be a good reason. From what she had seen, these people didn't do anything without a good reason.

The tall thug slid back the door to the rear compartment and she climbed inside. After securing the seat belt around her waist, he slid the door shut and yelled to the pilot to take off.

As soon as the chopper climbed to altitude, the sun burned through the smog and Sandra was able to see that they were heading south toward Mexico. The chopper seemed to be flying along the normal flight paths so she could only assume that it was on a routine flight plan, as if this was something it did all the time. So far, all the gang members she had seen were Anglos, Americans, but it was becoming obvious that they were headquartered in Mexico.

As soon as the chopper crossed the border, it dropped down low over the acres of squatters' huts and shanties and took a more evasive course, as if trying to evade the Mexican air traffic control radar. Before long, the chopper was over the empty desert, but still hugging the ground. The flight ended at a landing pad next to a large Mexican villa on the outskirts of what looked to be a small town. Several warehouses and buildings clustered around the villa were enclosed within a wire fence compound and the villa itself was surrounded with an additional wrought-iron security fence.

Two armed guards met her at the chopper and led her toward the villa. "What is this place?" she asked, but the guards didn't answer.

At the gate to the villa, one of the guards produced a plastic security card and opened the gate. Inside, one of the guards turned down a hallway while the other led her up to a room on the second floor and removed her restraints. "Wait here," he said in heavily accented English.

The door behind her opened and she turned to see who it was. "Lieutenant Miller!" Her eyes widened in shock when she saw who was behind this criminal operation. "What in the hell are you doing here?"

Miller smiled coldly, his eyes sliding past her scanty costume to fix on her face. "I could almost ask you the same thing," he said. "Except that I know exactly what you and Jennings were trying to pull."

"What do you mean?"

"You and Gunner thought that you'd hit the street to see if you could find out who is behind the helicopter bank robberies. You figured that it would help you clear yourself at the trial."

Sandra was speechless when the implications of what he had said sunk in. As the head of the investigation board, he had set her up and he was working for the gang.

"You found what you were looking for all right," Miller smiled thinly. "But I'm sorry to have to tell you that it isn't going to do you any good."

"What do you mean?"

"Well, for one thing," he said. "You're never going to stand trial. Your body will be found in a back alley in some border town and it'll look like you were the victim of a brutal sexual assault and murder."

Sandra was silent, a look of horror on her face.

"And," Miller continued, "don't think that Gunner is going to come to your rescue. He isn't going to live any longer than you are."

Amused by the look of shock on her face, Miller couldn't resist the urge to brag about what he had set up. After all, she was never going to have a chance to tell any of her cop buddies anything he had to say.

"You look surprised to hear this," he said. "Why do you think that the famous chopper cops can't seem to find their asses with both hands each time they come up against the Mangustas pulling those bank jobs? You were a pretty good left-hand seat systems operator as I remember," he smiled. "But when you ran into that Mangusta, you got ambushed like you were an amateur. Did you ever ask yourself why that happened that day? Why you didn't see that chopper in time?"

Sandra mutely shook her head.

"You didn't see it coming because it's a stealth chopper. Its countermeasure systems are set up to confuse your radars and sensors to give you false readings."

"But how?" she asked. "I thought that couldn't be done."

"You're a pretty good systems operator," he repeated. "But you don't know much about counter-measures. Actually, it was easy, they just installed jammers that had been specifically designed to operate on the Griffin's frequencies."

"And you gave them the frequencies."

"Sure, why not? They recognize talent in a man when they see it and they pay me well."

"Who is this 'they' you keep talking about?"

"The people I work for," Miller smiled. "I guess you'd say that they are into pharmaceuticals."

Sandra's mind clicked back to the Frienzia Pharmaceutical badge on the door of the chopper that had brought her here. Now she knew the tie-in. Frienzia was manufacturing 'edge'.

Sandra didn't like the way Miller kept eyeing the large amount of her exposed bare skin. "Could you get me something else to wear?" she asked him. "It's getting chilly in here."

"I wouldn't worry about that," he said without smiling. "You're not going to have much use for clothes while you're here."

When Sandra didn't answer, he smirked. "Don't you want to know why you won't need them?"

"I can figure that part out," she said, looking at him like she would at a fresh dog turd stuck on the bottom of her shoe.

"Oh," he smiled. "I'm sure that you know part of it, but all you know is the grand finale. You don't have any idea what's going to happen to you before I finally get into that stuck-up little pussy of yours. Before I'm done with you, bitch, you're going to be down on your hands and knees begging for it. I'm really going to enjoy seeing that," he said. "That's going to be a lot more fun than actually screwing you. Sandra Revell, the queen bitch chopper cop who thinks that she's such hot shit, begging for a man to stick it in her. I'm going to love it."

There was nothing for Sandra to say, so she just stared straight into his eyes.

"But," he continued, glancing down at his watch, "sorry to say, this is all going to have to wait for a while. As you can imagine, I'm a busy man. So, as much as I hate to, I'm going to have to put this off for a while. But don't worry," he laughed. "I'm not going to forget about you."

CHAPTER 20

Rio del Sangre, Mexico

Miller's laughter rang in Sandra's ears as he walked out of the room. No sooner had he cleared the door before two guards came in, their weapons drawn, and escorted her to a small bedroom across the hall. Sandra heard the lock click behind her as she looked around the room.

A brass-framed bed dominated the small room, with a dressing table to the right of it. A small bath was off on the left and two curtained windows looked down onto the grounds below. It was a marked improvement over her last temporary prison, but it was not going to be any easier to escape from. The windows were barred and the lock on the door was sheathed with a metal plate.

After examining her cell, she kicked off her shoes and lay down on the bed. But even though she closed her eyes, she wasn't able to relax. Her mind flashed back to that last night in the Denver Club before they had flown to LA. She had jumped in Wolff and Gunner's shit that night for having gotten ambushed by the Mangustas outside of Reno like a couple of rookies.

Now she knew that it hadn't been their fault, but there was no way that she could let them know that. There was no way that she could warn them that each time they encountered the

Mangustas they would be flying into an ambush, because Miller had revealed their weaknesses and the Griffins were flying totally blind.

Worry about Dragon Flight forced Sandra's mind away from dwelling on her own situation. She knew that Miller was coming back. And, while she didn't know the exact details, she had a pretty good idea what he was planning to do to her before he killed her. And she knew that being raped was not going to be the worst part of it. Every woman feared being raped, but Sandra feared it less than other women who did not have her well-honed skills of self-defense. She knew that she was more than able to defend herself against any man who was less of a martial arts expert than she was.

The problem was that Miller was well aware of what she was capable of doing if her hands and feet were free. There was no way that he was going to give her even the slightest chance to defend herself against him. He would be sure to have her tied up, or beaten senseless or both, before he finally raped her. That much she was sure of.

Sandra was a realist. She knew that she would be raped if she didn't resist. She also knew that she would still be raped if she did resist. The only difference was that she would be beaten into submission first. And, while she knew that she could survive being raped, she was not so sure that she would survive being badly beaten if she tried to resist.

Therefore, she had no other choice; she had to allow Miller to violate her without resisting him in any way. Even the thought of him touching her was repugnant, but she had to be realistic.

If she had been captured by someone who didn't know her, there was always the possibility that she could playact enough to make him think that she welcomed his attentions to escape being tied up or beaten until she could get away. But with Miller there was no fucking way that he was going to buy a line like that. He knew exactly what she thought of him. He was never going to think that she would accept being sexually humiliated. He knew better than that.

It was obvious that Miller was completely psychotic, and he was probably a practicing sadist on top of that. She wondered how he had been able to slip past the psychological tests to get into the Tac Force. Or maybe he had acquired a taste for rape after he had joined the force. If she survived this, she was going to have to take a look at his personnel file and see what had gone wrong.

If she survived.

In the movies, the heroine always got away from her attacker at the last dramatic moment, but this wasn't the movies. As a cop, she knew that was not the way it worked in real life. Rarely did a woman escape from a man who had captured her. Not, at least, before she had been raped at least once. It was going to happen and there was very little she could do about it.

She only hoped that she could survive the ordeal without being badly hurt.

By the time Wolff got back down to the flight line, the 25mm chain gun had been mounted in Dragon One Zero's nose turret. Mugabe was helping Red's armament people do the last of the firing circuit checks when the pilot walked up to him.

"What'd you find out?" Mojo asked.

Wolff waved a thick computer printout at him. "There's more of those damned things in LA than I thought were still in existence. With the gas guzzler tax, I thought all of the old Caddies had gone to the junkyards long ago."

"Maybe this is where all the old Detroit lead sleds come to die."

"That's what it looks like," Wolff said. "But they aren't dying fast enough."

"How many red ones did you find?"

"Fifty-six red, twenty-three orange, and eighteen maroon late-model Caddies," Wolff said. "And we've got to check out each and every last one of them."

Mojo snapped the inspection panel back in place. "We'd better get on it then."

"Before we do that," Wolff said, "the first thing we need to do is to march this list over to our hosts and see if we can get one of them to run the registration on all of these plates for us. This is just a rough DMV list. Mom didn't have time to sort through them."

"Hadn't you better brief that replacement crew first?" Mojo reminded him. "You don't want Buzz on your ass about something else."

"Oh, shit," Wolff said, folding the computer runout and stuffing it in the side pocket of his flight suit. "I almost forgot about them. Where are they?"

"Last I saw, they were having their ears bent by Red."

"Oh, shit! I'd better get them away from him before he gets them all sorts of fucked up."

Knox and Gordon, the replacement fliers, were as glad to get away from Red as Wolff was to rescue them. "I'm Rick Wolff," he said, extending his hand. "The Dragon Flight leader."

He nodded toward Mojo. "And that's Jumal Mugabe, my gunner."

Knox, the pilot, took his hand and introduced himself and his gunner. "What happened to the two guys we're replacing?" he asked.

"It was only one guy, the other one was a woman cop, and it's a long story," Wolff replied. "But I'll fill you in while I show you to your palatial quarters."

Gunner had almost passed out from the pain in his arms

by the time someone came to get him. His hands were swollen and the steel bands of the cuffs were half buried in his blue flesh by the time they were unlocked. The pain of the blood flushing back into his hands was excruciating, and he bit his lip to keep from crying out as his guards led him out into the light.

He was taken to a large modern building across the chopper pad from the hangar. The place looked like a manufacturing facility of some kind and he wondered if the Frienzia Pharmaceutical logo he had seen on the chopper that had brought him here was legit. He had a gut feeling that it was. What would be a better cover for an illegal drug manufacturing operation than to hide it in a legal pharmaceutical manufacturing facility?

His guards led him into a side door that opened onto a hallway with offices on each side. They stopped at the end of the hall and knocked on a polished mahogany door before opening it. The large suite inside had all the earmarks of an executive's office: wood-paneled walls, a polished conference table, and a huge oak desk at the end of the room. An older man sat in a leather chair at the desk while a younger man stood slightly off to his left side. Both of them wore blank shirts, white ties, and expensive silk suits that bulged in the left armpit.

He had finally learned who was behind both the Mangustas and 'edge'—the Mafia. But he didn't think that the information was going to do him any good.

"You're a chopper cop, right," the man behind the desk said.

"I was," Gunner corrected him. "But I was kicked off the force last week."

Gunner gave him a slightly modified version of what had happened at the shooting board investigation. His version of the story ended with him being dismissed for bad-mouthing Buzz and the board about Sandra's verdict. He was taking a risk in doing that if, as he believed, they had a chopper cop on their payroll. But it was all he could think of at the moment, and it was better than telling them the truth.

"And you want to get into the drug business?"

Gunner shrugged and tried to smile. "A man's got to make a living somehow."

The mafioso didn't senile back. "The woman who was with you, what does she think?"

"Like I said," Gunner reminded him, "she's the reason I got kicked out. I've worked with her for a couple of years and we're real tight. She does what I say."

That wasn't a complete fabrication. Sandra had done what he had suggested since they had started this dumb-ass undercover stunt.

The mafioso studied him for a long moment. "You will stay with us tonight; there's someone I want you to talk to tomorrow."

"Sure," Gunner said as if he had any other choice. "And the girl?"

"I wouldn't worry about her right now, if I were you. She's being well taken care of."

There was nothing he could say to that, so he didn't even try. The guards led him back out into the hallway and down to a small room with a steel door. Inside, the room was bare but for a cot, a sink, and a toilet. Gunner went in and sat on the cot as the door was locked behind him.

If Gunner needed any further identification as to who his captors were it was answered a few minutes later when one of his guards brought him his dinner—a plate of spaghetti covered with a thin tomato sauce and a thick slice of bread. The food smelled good and he dove right in. He had been running all day on just a couple cups of coffee and was starved.

As he sopped up the last of the sauce with the bread, he realized that if they were willing to feed him, it meant that there was still a chance that he was going to live.

* * *

As soon as he had the new men settled in, Wolff went to the LAPD office and was able to talk one of the officers into showing them how to run the plates on one of their spare computer terminals in the office. In only slightly more time than it took to punch in the license plate numbers, the computer spit out the data on each Caddy's registered owner and the location of the car itself.

As the list came out of the printer, Mojo quickly went over the names, eliminating the Caddies driven by little old ladies, those in the wrecking yards, those in the police impound yards and those abandoned in the gridlocked freeway sections. When they were done, there were only a little over three dozen late model Caddies that had not been accounted for.

"There," Mojo said as he hit the key to print out the revised list. "It's a little more workable now, but that's still a hell of a lot of cars."

"No sweat," Wolff said. "We'll start in on it as soon as we go on patrol this evening."

Finding a particular car in a place like LA was like trying to find a particular grain of sand on the beach. It was close to impossible, but impossible or not, it would be much easier to do it from the air.

"What are we going to do when we find them?" Mojo asked.

"Hell, Mojo, you know the drill," Wolff said. "Stop them, ask them for their registration, shine a light in their eyes, and ask them to open their trunk."

Mojo shook his head. "You're talking about making profile stops with a Griffin, aren't you?"

Making profile stops was the once-controversial practice where a police officer would follow the feeling in his gut and stop a car just because he felt that something was wrong. The car or the driver fit a profile of a certain type of criminal behavior hence the name.

In the eighties, the criminal defense lawyers had screamed about constitutional rights each time one of their maggot clients got nailed on a profile stop, but the tactic had proved so valuable that every police force in the nation now used it. And, while the public defenders still didn't like it, the Supreme Court had finally bowed to common sense and had ruled profile stops to be a legitimate weapon in the battle against crime.

"You got a better idea?"

"Nope."

"Then let's get on with it."

CHAPTER 21

Torrance Airfield, Los Angeles

As Mojo was pre-flighting the Griffin for the evening patrol, he thought of something he could do that would cut some of the odds against them. "Have you got that printout?" he asked Wolff. "The original one that shows where all those cars are?"

"Sure," Wolff said, reaching into the pocket behind his seat and pulling it out. "Why?"

Mojo quickly ran down the list. "I've got an idea that may save us a lot of time."

"What's that?"

Mojo found what he wanted and noted an address. "Let's fly over to the East LA impound yard. They've got a Caddy in there and I want to make some calibration runs on it."

"Good idea."

At the yard, it was easy for Mojo to talk the LAPD officers into letting him run sensor tests on the '94 Caddy he found in their yard. He didn't know the model year of the car he and Wolff had seen Legs get into, but the '94 Caddy would be similar if not identical for his purposes.

As the Griffin hovered overhead, one of the officers started the car's engine, let it come up to operating temperature, and then drove it around in traffic while Mojo and Wolff followed it. As they flew above it, Mojo tracked it with his sensors and determined its particular heat emission pattern and the way in which it showed up on the Doppler radar and magnetic anomaly detectors.

After ten minutes of this, he had all the data on the car that he needed and stored it in the chopper's computer. Now, any time that the sensors picked up this specific pattern, they would lock on and sound an alarm. Armed with that data, it was time to go Caddy hunting.

With the chopper's mirror skin dialed to matte dead black, all the navigation lights turned off, and the rotor blades set to fine pitch, the Griffin was almost invisible and was as silent as it could be without mounting the special turbine noise-suppression kits. The kits had been left behind in Denver or Wolff would have added them, too. But, as it was, the streets of LA were noisy enough that the background din masked the sound of the chopper almost as well.

From fifteen hundred feet in the night sky, the streets of LA were a patchwork of lights, most of them moving. In fact, enough of the streetlamps were burned out that in some areas, the only way they could tell where the streets were was to follow the stream of traffic.

They had been cruising for almost an hour when a red light on the sensor console started blinking. Mojo punched up the target data and studied it for a second. "We have a target at eight hundred meters heading east."

"Copy," Wolff said as he banked the Griffin around to the new heading. "Give me the data"

Wolff's HUD, the Heads Up Display, came on with the target information illuminated on the inside of the canopy at eye level. A glowing blue map showed the cars moving on the streets below, and a pulsing red light was centered on the subject vehicle.

Rolling back on the throttle to cut his airspeed, Wolff

dropped down over the Caddy several meters behind but still keeping pace with it. In the scattered, dim light of the streetlamps, he could not tell if the car was red, orange, or maroon, but it definitely was a late-model Caddy.

"You ready?" he called over to Mojo.

The gunner switched on the external loudspeakers and armed the weapons in the nose turret. The 40mm grenade launcher was feeding stun gas rounds and the 25mm was set on the single shot mode and was feeding AP ammunition. One of those rounds through an engine would stop a car in its tracks.

"Let's do it."

Wolff cut his throttle even more and dropped down only a few meters above the car but still keeping far back to its rear. Mojo hit the switch for the external speakers and keyed his throat mike. "Driver of the Cadillac sedan heading east on Ventura. This is the United States Tactical Police Force. Stop your car and get out slowly with your hands in the air."

Mojo had barely finished his message when the Caddy took off in a cloud of burning rubber. He could see the driver turning to look out the windscreen trying to see who or what was talking to him.

"Do we have probable cause?" he asked with a grin.

"Damned straight," Wolff answered, giving the classic reason for making a profile stop. "He's got his license plate light burned out."

"Let's do it."

Wolff cracked the throttle, and the turbines screamed as the Griffin shot forward passing low over the top of the Caddy. A hundred meters in front of it, he kicked down on the rudder pedal and snapped the tail around so that they were facing the oncoming car. Before Wolff had even completed the turn, Mojo flipped the switch to the million candlepower Nite Sun searchlights under the chopper's nose.

The sudden blaze of light all but blinded the driver.

Throwing his hands up to cover his face, the car ran up over the curb and headed into a burned-out lamppost. The left front wheel tried to climb up the lamppost and the Caddy rolled over onto its right side as it skidded to a crashing halt against a parked car.

The driver kicked open his door and staggered out of the wreckage, a pistol in his hand. Mojo didn't even bother to tell him to put it down; he just triggered off a short burst of 40mm stun gas grenades.

The instant the faintly green gas enveloped him, the driver dropped to the pavement as if he had been hit in the head with a baseball bat. As he brought the chopper in for a landing next to the Caddy, Wolff got on the horn to the LAPD to report the incident.

A patrol car was soon on the scene and took custody of the prisoner on the charge of threatening a federal officer with a firearm.

The next Caddy they came across tried to make a run for it, too. But this time, they vectored it into an LAPD roadblock. A search of the car revealed a load of drugs in the trunk and a pistol under the front seat.

Midway through their four-hour patrol, Wolff and Mojo had nailed five Caddies and their drivers had all been lodged in the holding cells at the LA Field Office for interrogation in the morning.

Wolff called in a Code Seven for fifteen—a coffee break—from a parking lot next to a 7-Eleven. Mojo walked over to get two large cups of coffee while Wolff stayed with the ship. Leaving the chopper unguarded in LA was an open invitation to having it trashed, or stolen.

"It's been fun hunting land barges," Mojo said, sipping his weak coffee. "But I'm not sure that we're going about this the right way. We're nailing Caddies, but we're not getting any closer to finding Legs and Gunner."

"How's that?"

"Well, we aren't targeting the right Caddy owners."

"Say what?" Wolff exclaimed. "Over half of the guys we've stopped have been packing, and two of them shot at us."

"Yes, but just because some guy's packing iron doesn't mean that he's the guy we're looking for."

"You've got a point there," Wolff admitted.

"The way I figure it," Mojo continued, "Gunner and Legs decided that they'd do a little undercover work, that's why she was dressed that way. And we saw her getting into the Caddy in a notorious drug-dealing area. So, it seems to me that a good place to look for our lead is to go downtown where we saw her the other night."

"Sounds good to me," Wolff said as he dropped his empty styro-foam cup into the trash bag behind the seats. He glanced down at his watch. "We've still got a couple of hours before we're off duty. Let's do it."

Mojo threw back the last of his coffee. "Let's."

The Griffin was over the deserted downtown area in just a matter of minutes. Wolff throttled back and cruised back and forth over the area at two thousand feet so that even the faint sound of the rotors would not reach the ground as Mojo studied his sensor console. There was no shortage of cars on the dimly lit streets below, but no Caddies. Mojo had Wolff open up his orbit to take in more of the area below. "Bingo!" Mojo said suddenly. "I think I've got one."

"Show me."

Mojo flashed the data onto Wolff's HUD. The car was coming up a side street leading onto the boulevard running between the abandoned skyscrapers. "It matches the pattern for a Caddy sedan," he said.

"Let's talk to him," Wolff said as he cut his pitch and maneuvered the Griffin down lower in between the tall buildings to take up a position right above and slightly behind the moving car.

The Caddy was just rounding the corner onto the boulevard when Mojo keyed his mike. "Cadillac sedan moving north on Wilshire, this is the United States Tactical Police. Stop your car and..."

A winking orange-red light appeared from the open driver's window of the car. "The bastard's firing at us!"

"Waste him," Wolff snapped.

Mojo had already locked in the turret weapons, so a squeeze from his right forefinger fired a single 25mm round down through the Caddy's hood. The AP round punched through the hood and shattered the engine block below.

The car stopped dead in its tracks, but before the driver could get out, Mojo sent a brief volley of stun gas grenades down. The driver collapsed with the door only halfway open.

Landing the chopper in a flurry of dust and trash, Mojo leaped from his door, pulling his pistol as he ran. The whores and druggies had fled deeper into the night when the first shot had been fired, so the gunner had the street all to himself as he dragged the driver out of the car and slapped the cuffs on him.

Reaching into the car, he scooped up the driver's weapon, an Uzi submachine gun, and slung it over his shoulder. Taking the keys from the ignition, he opened the trunk and found the dealer's stock in trade, about a kilogram of 'edge' in small Baggies stacked in a nylon travel bag.

When he signaled to Wolff, the pilot stepped down out of the cockpit with the spray can of stun gas antidote in his hand. A quick spray in the driver's face soon brought him around and he woke to see Mojo and Wolff bending over him, their pistols in their hands.

After introducing themselves and reading him his rights, Mojo started questioning him. "Last night," Mojo said, "a blond woman in a short skirt and see-through blouse got into the backseat of your Caddy. Where'd you take her?"

"I don't know nothin' 'bout no white ho'," he said

sullenly. "There be white hos all over down here."

"We saw her get into your car," Mojo said.

"They be no ho' gettin' in my ride last night."

"This maggot's lying to us," Mojo stated flatly.

"Is he now?" Wolff smiled tightly as he caught Mojo's eyes. "Maybe he'd like to talk to us in the air."

"Good idea."

Mojo grabbed the man's arm and started dragging him toward the Griffin. "Hey, man," he shouted. "What you be doin'?"

"You be goin' fo' a ride, Blood," Mojo said.

Mojo usually spoke standard American English. It was only when he got angry that he lapsed into the black street dialect he had learned as a child.

"What you mean, man! I ain't gettin' in no fuckin' chopper."

Mojo spun him around and slammed him up against the side door of the Griffin. "You think you one bad-ass nigger, don't you," Mojo snarled, his face just inches from the dealer's. "But I be the baddest nigger you ever did see. You an' me, we be goin' in there and we gonna talk while this honkey flies this thing as high as he can go. I don' like what you saying, I be throwing yo' sorry black ass out."

The dealer's eyes rolled back and he looked as if he were about to pass out.

"You got that, bro?"

The dealer nodded.

"You got anythin' to tell me now?"

It was all Mojo could do to get the guy to shut up so they could put him in the car that came to transport him down to the field office.

Right before midnight in the LA Tac Force field office,

Jim Miller was going over the evening's after-action reports when he came across the results of Wolff and Mojo's Caddy-hunting expedition. Of the names of the five men they had put in the holding cells, one of them caught his attention. Pickett, Roland R., was one of his second-level street distributors. The report didn't say anything about his having been questioned by Wolff, but Miller couldn't afford to take a chance on it.

The problem was that Pickett was being held on the charge of possessing an automatic weapon. Wolff had nabbed him with an Uzi, a clear violation of the federal firearm statutes and one that did not allow bail under any circumstances. So there was no point in him calling in the public defender to see about getting him sprung on bail. Roland would have to have his accident in jail. He punched up the screen showing who was being held in custody, studied it for a moment, and then exited the screen. Reaching into his desk drawer, he pulled out two packs of cigarettes and put them in his pocket before getting to his feet. It was easier to do it here anyway.

CHAPTER 22

Torrance Airfield, Los Angeles

Considering how late they had been up the night before, Wolff and Mojo were up quite early the next morning. "What do you want to do today?" Mojo asked Wolff over coffee.

"The first thing I think we need to do is to check out that motel room and see if we can find that supplier our man told us about last night."

"Good idea," Mojo agreed. "You want to talk to the field office or do it ourselves?"

Wolff thought for a moment. "Let's do it ourselves," he said. "We can take them downtown ourselves if we find out anything."

After telling Mom where they were going, they borrowed a car from the LA office and drove over to the Raging Surf Motel and parked the car close to the office. Making sure that their pistols were loaded and off safety, they slowly approached room 12.

Wolff and Mojo could smell the blood before they even knocked on the door. So could the flies, and they swarmed, waiting for the door to be opened. Wolff tried the handle and the door pushed open. The stench hit him like a hammer and he turned away.

Mojo pushed past him, his pistol ready even though there was clearly no need for it. The inside of the room looked like a slaughterhouse. Blood splattered the faded paint on the walls like a paisley print and puddled deeply in clotted masses on the bed and floor. From the bright-red color, he knew that the blood was only a few hours old.

The body of a nude man lay on the floor, a sock stuffed in his mouth and his hands bound behind him. Because of all of the wounds to his torso, it was difficult to tell how he had died, but, from the congealing puddle of blood between his legs, he seemed to have bled to death from a wound to the genitals. Looking closer, Mojo saw that he had been castrated.

The body of what looked like a teenage girl lay spread-eagled on the bed, her hands and feet tied to the bedposts. It was easy to see what had killed her. Or at least what had finally killed her. Her belly had been ripped open from crotch to breastbone. Before that, she had been cut to ribbons and had probably been raped, but from the extent of the wounds to her vaginal area, it would be difficult to tell without an autopsy.

Wolff poked his head in through the door. "Is that our man?"

Mojo shook his head as he backed out of the room. "Hard to tell, but I've got a feeling that it is."

"Shit!"

At the motel's office, Wolff laid his badge on the counter. The clerk's eyes flicked down to it and back up, "What can I do to help you, Officer?"

"Call the police and an ambulance. You've got two bodies in room 12."

The clerk seemed totally unconcerned by Wolff's request. Apparently, this wasn't the first time that someone had been murdered in one of his rooms.

The police responded quickly, the first car arriving in less than ten minutes. "What d' ya got?" the LA detective asked after they exchanged identifications and names.

"A couple of bodies pretty well chopped up," Wolff said. "We think the guy was a drug supplier."

"Let's take a look."

"Ah, shit!" the detective shook his head when he saw the bodies. "We've got another one of them."

"Another one of what?" Mojo asked.

"We've got some maniac on the loose who keeps doing this shit," the detective answered. "We get one of these every couple of weeks."

"Any idea what's behind them?"

"Na." The detective was obviously bored and didn't really give a shit why these people had been killed. Dozens of people died every day in LA and more than half of them died violently. "All of the victims are tied into the drug trade somehow and the brass feels that it's a turf war gone bad."

Wolff glanced over at the girl's remains. "Not a sex murderer?"

"Nope," the cop shook his head. "Sometimes it's just a guy, or two queers."

"What are the tox screens on the other victims showing?" Mojo asked.

"The usual shit," the detective answered. He stopped and thought for a moment. "The funny thing is, though, that they've all tested positive for 'edge'. And that doesn't make any sense. 'Edge' isn't like coke or ice, it doesn't turn you whacko."

"Are you picking up any prints?"

The detective shook his head. "That's why we think it's a drug war. Whoever's doing this is psycho for sure, but he's a real pro. He never leaves a thing behind." The cop looked back at the bed. "Other than bodies, that is."

"What's the Tac Force's interest in this case?" he asked. "I didn't hear anything about you guys doing a drug investigation here."

Wolff jumped right in. He didn't want this getting back to Buzz before he had a chance to think about it. "We had a tip from an informant and thought this guy could help us with another investigation."

"You were hoping he could 'assist you with your inquiries,' as the Brits put it?"

"Something like that."

The detective looked skeptical, but he didn't ask any more questions. The chopper cops were turning up all the time and it was best if the local cops didn't get too involved with what they were doing.

Wolff and Mojo stayed until the forensic team had gone over the bodies and bagged them, but nothing of interest was found. After exchanging phone numbers with the detective, they got back in their borrowed car and drove off.

"What do we do now?" Wolff asked as he pulled out into traffic.

Mugabe shook his head slowly. "Damned if I know," he said. "But we can always go back and try to talk to the guy we picked up last night. Maybe he'll be a little more informative if he knows what happened to his supplier here."

"Let's do it."

The desk sergeant at the Field Office looked up from his computer screen. "What can I do for you guys?" Wolff laid his badge out. "Lieutenant Wolff and Sergeant Mugabe. We'd like to talk to that dealer we brought in last night, Pickett, Roland R."

The desk sergeant entered the name into the computer. "Sorry 'bout that, guys," he said. "Pickett checked out early this morning."

"What do you mean checked out?' Wolff said. "I had that maggot in here on a federal weapons charge hold."

"'Checked out' as in died," the sergeant explained.

"Right after Lieutenant Miller interrogated him last night, someone shut him up permanently."

"How?"

A ballpoint pen driven through the ear into the brain."

Wolff and Mugabe exchanged looks, a classic jailhouse execution. What in the hell was going on here?

"Is Miller in?" Wolff asked.

The sergeant looked over at the sign-out board by the door. "Nope, he's signed out till late this afternoon. Can someone else help you?"

"No thanks, I'll talk to him later."

When Wolff and Mojo left the Field Office, they walked back to their car. "Now what are we going to do?" Wolff asked, the key poised to go into the ignition switch. "We just lost our only connection to Gunner and Legs."

"Have you noticed," Mojo asked, "how many times Jim Miller's name keeps popping up in all of this?"

"What you mean?"

"Well for one thing, he was the guy in charge of an investigation that should have cleared Legs, not brought her up on charges. Secondly, after she's been charged, he stops off to give Buzz a raft of shit and at the same time rubs our faces in the fact that we haven't been able to find those Mangustas. Now we learn that he talks to the man we bring in and our man is killed immediately thereafter. Wouldn't you say that that's starting to stretch credulity there?"

"But he's one of us," Wolff said. "He's a gold-plated asshole, sure, but he's still Tac Force."

Mojo raised one eyebrow. "Lucifer was an angel, too. And, according to the story, he sat at the right hand of God."

"What are you saying?"

"What I'm saying is that just because he's Tac Force doesn't mean that he's clean. Remember, it had to have been someone on the inside who gave the bad guys our sensor data and made this whole thing possible."

Wolff thought for a moment. "The guy's a real prick all right, and as much as I'd like to, I just don't know if I can see him as the traitor."

Mojo stared off into the distance for a brief second. "There's something else," he said, "that may have a bearing on this. It involves Legs and that's why I've never mentioned it before."

That got Wolff's fullest attention. "What's that?"

"You remember that Legs came on board right before Miller shipped out to come down here?"

"Vaguely."

"Well, anyway, Miller started hitting on her almost from the first day she started working with us. She was trying so hard to be just another one of the guys—you know how she is about that—that she just put up with it instead of kicking him right in the balls."

Wolff's face grew hard. "I didn't know anything about that."

"Not too many people did, but, anyway, one night I was hanging around the base, you were off at that Leadership Academy if I remember right..."

"What a bunch of bullshit that was."

"...Anyway, I went into the locker room to get something out of my locker when I heard the two of them talking on the other side of the room. I could hear that she was pissed about something and I figured that she had to be pissed at him, so I stayed back out of sight in case it got nasty and she needed some help."

Mojo chuckled. "It turned out that she didn't need any help from me. The next thing I heard was a thud and Miller crying out. She said something about him keeping his fucking hands to himself and stomped out of the room. I peeked around the corner of a locker and saw Miller on the floor clutching his balls. Apparently she had finally put the knee to him and did it good."

Wolff's face broke out in a smile. "Good girl."

"Anyway," Mojo concluded, "I backed on out of the room quietly and kept it to myself. I knew that Miller was leaving right away and I didn't see any purpose in reporting it and making trouble for him about it."

He paused. "Now, though, I'm beginning to wonder if he isn't tied into all of this somehow."

"I wouldn't mind thinking so," Wolff admitted. "But there are too many loose ends that need to be tied up before we can point a finger at him."

"Like?"

"'Edge'," Wolff said. "How does it fit into all of this and how is he tied into it?"

"What do you mean?"

"Well, it seems that everywhere we go with this, we find that drug involved. Like, why did Legs and Gunner go to 'edge' dealers to try to get information about the Mangustas? That doesn't make much sense to me."

Mojo thought for a moment. "Maybe it does after all," he said slowly. "Think about it. Whoever's flying those choppers has got to have a big-time organization behind them, and what's more big time than drugs? Particularly a new, popular drug called 'edge.'"

"But if they're working for a drug cartel, why are they knocking over banks?"

"That's the part that beats the shit outta me," Mojo shrugged. "Maybe they're just doing it for thrills."

Wolff shook his head. "No. That can't be it. A big organization doesn't do anything just for thrills, not if they want to stay in business. If the 'edge' organization is behind the Mangustas, there's a damned good reason for what they're doing."

"So where does that leave us?"

Wolff shrugged. "It leaves us with shit. We don't have any more leads now than we did when we first got here." He paused. "And we've still got Legs and Gunner missing."

"But we still have Miller," Mojo insisted.

"But how is Miller tied into this theory of yours?"

Mojo was silent for a long moment. "I don't really know," he said slowly. "I only know that he is."

"Buzz isn't going to buy your gut feeling," Wolff said. "Not as sufficient probable cause for busting a Tac Force lieutenant. We can't pull a profile stop on Miller."

"That's why we're going to have to keep an eye on that guy ourselves until we can put something together that'll hold up in court."

"But only after we've found Legs and Gunner," Wolff insisted.

CHAPTER 23

Tijuana, Mexico

Gunner was wide awake when the guards came in to get him early that morning. He had slept through the night and had awakened at his usual time, ready for his first cup of coffee of the morning. When the guards came, however, it was not to invite him out for coffee. Their pistols drawn, they ordered him to put his hands behind his back and slipped a set of plastic restraints over his wrists.

After unnecessarily patting him down, they led him down to the executive office at the end of the hall. The same two black-shirt, white-tie types he had met the afternoon before were there, as well as another man who frequented the same tailor.

"You've got a problem, asshole," the man behind the desk said. "I found out that you lied to me."

"How's that?"

"You and that woman are working undercover."

"That's bullshit," Gunner said. "I told you that they kicked me off the force. Everyone knows that."

"You resigned because your co-pilot, that woman with you," the mafioso glanced down at a paper on his desk, "—Sandra Revell, was suspended for shooting up some old lady."

Gunner was stunned. Unlike the results of the shooting

board investigation, his resignation wasn't public knowledge. These guys had to have an informant inside the Tac Force, maybe even inside Dragon Flight itself.

"You look surprised, Gunner," came the voice behind him. "You should have known better than to think we'd fall for a line of shit like that."

"Miller!" Gunner said, turning around. The TPF officer was wearing his duty uniform and the slight smirk that Gunner had come to expect from him. "I should have known that you were involved in this shit."

"You aren't smart enough to figure out something like that." Miller smirked. "You always were a pretty stupid bastard."

If Gunner's hands had been free, he would have gone for Miller's throat. But, as it was, he could only stand there and take it. "What now?" he asked.

Miller smiled. "What now? What do you think, asshole. You're going for a little ride."

"What about Sandra?" Gunner asked as the guards grasped his arms to lead him away.

"Don't worry about your girlfriend," Miller said with a smile. "I'm going to take real good care of her. You might even say that I'm going to give her what she's been needing all these years."

Gunner struggled to turn around to face Miller again.

"You motherfucker," he snarled. "You touch her and I'll cut your balls off."

Miller stepped up to him, his face contorted with rage. "Don't you threaten me, asshole," he snarled as he savagely slammed his fist into Gunner's stomach. "You're not going to do anything but die."

The pilot doubled up with the blow. Miller hit him again, driving his fist into his mouth, splitting his lips. Gunner fell to his knees.

"That's enough, Miller!" the head mafioso snapped.

Miller stepped back as Gunner's guards hauled him back up to his feet.

"Get him out of here," the mafioso ordered.

Licking the blood from his smashed lips, Gunner took a last, long look at Miller. "I'm not going to forget you, motherfucker."

Miller's laughter rang in his ears as the guards hauled Gunner away.

Back at the airfield, Wolff went into the CP and found Mom sitting at her usual place behind her commo console. "Ruby," he said. "Could you have your number two take over here for a moment, I'd like to talk to you."

Mom looked up in surprise. Wolff never called her by her name unless something was wrong, very wrong. "Sure, Wolf, just a second."

Calling the other commo tech to come over to take her place, she got up and followed the pilot outside to the tarmac. "What's up?" she asked.

Wolff quickly filled her in on what had happened on their Caddy hunt the night before and what they had found this morning when they had tried to follow-up on their information.

"Have you reported this to Buzz?"

Wolff shook his head. "He's not interested in listening to me right now, he's still all sorts of pissed off about Reno. I can't go to him with this until I can come up with something solid."

"What do you want me to do?"

"Miller," he said simply. "I want you to help me get the goods on Jim Miller."

Mom frowned. "Why him?"

Wolff quickly went over all the coincidences involving Miller and the events of the last few days. He even briefed her on the stealth choppers and how they had been able to jam the

Griffin's sensors. Washington was still keeping the security lid on that information, but Wolff knew that Mom would keep it to herself.

"I never liked him, either," she said, shaking her head. "But I don't know about this."

"Damnit, Mom," Wolff said. "I know he's Tac Force, but that doesn't mean that he's clean. For Christ's sakes, we've had our share of assholes in the force over the years."

"But a traitor?"

"Why not, there always has to be a first."

"Okay," she said reluctantly. "I'll see what I can dig up on him."

"Thanks, Mom."

"I can't guarantee anything, but I'll try."

"Check into his bank balance," Wolff suggested. "Find out if he has a passport. Find out what he drives and where he lives."

"I know what to do, Wolff," Mom snapped.

"Sorry, I was just trying to help."

"I'll do what I can."

"Thanks."

"But I think you're wrong."

"I sure as hell hope not," he said. "'Cause he's the last lead we have. Legs and Gunner are out there somewhere and we can't find them."

"I know," Mom said softly. "That's the only reason I'm going to do this."

Wolff watched her walk back into the CP. If there was anyone in the United States who could tap into the real Jim Miller it was Mom. She knew ways to dig information out of inaccessible places that not even the CIA were aware of. Miller's life was recorded in some computer somewhere and Mom could get any computer in the nation to talk to her if she worked on the access codes long enough.

He turned and walked toward Red's office. He felt an urgent need to fry his brain with a cup of Red's coffee—maybe it would stir up the gray matter a little and give him a new idea to work on. God only knew, he had fuck-all to go on right now. Red had his feet up on his desk and the ever-present cigar stuffed in his face. He looked up when Wolff walked in but didn't greet him; his attention was focused on the radar manual he was reading. Wolff sorted through the clutter on the top of the filing cabinet until he found the cleanest of the dirty cups and poured himself half a cup.

He didn't fear contagion from drinking out of the crusty cup—Red's brew could kill anything short of the HIV virus. He refrained, however, from adding any of the powdered creamer to his coffee; it always made the brew turn a sickly shade of green and it was still a little too early in the day for green coffee.

Red looked up when Wolff sat down on the edge of his desk. "Git yer ass off my desk!" he snarled before going back to his reading. Red read new maintenance manuals the way other people devoured skin magazines.

Wolff stood back up and took a sip of his coffee. When he continued to hold his silence, Red looked up from the manual again.

"What do you want, for Christ's sakes?" he snapped.

"The benefit of your age and wisdom."

"Smartass," Red growled.

"No," Wolff said. "I mean it. I need help trying to find Legs and Gunner."

When Red put the manual down, Wolff quickly filled him in on what he and Mojo had tried to do and where it had ended at both the motel and the Field Office holding cells.

"And you think that Miller's wrapped up in all this?" was Red's only comment.

"Yes, I do," Wolff answered. "I just don't know how to prove it."

"If you really think so," Red said, "why don't you talk to him about it? Give him your story and see what he has to say for himself."

That was one way to do it: go head-to-head with him and see what happened. "There's only one problem with that," Wolff said. "He's out of the office today. Something about a meeting with the Mexican authorities."

"Find out when he's coming back," Red suggested. "Set up an appointment with him. Make him wonder why you want to talk to him. Put him on the defensive instead of merely reacting to what's happening on this case."

Wolff smiled. "Maybe I can do that. Thanks, Red."

The maintenance chief was already back in his radar manual and only grunted in reply.

When Sandra woke and saw that the sun was up, she knew that she had slept through the night. She had been relieved of her watch so she didn't know exactly what time it was, but her stomach told her that it was well past breakfast time. Her dinner last night had been only a small plate of Spanish rice and chicken, so she was hungry.

Getting out of bed, she went to the door and listened, but she heard nothing in the hall outside. While she still had time, she went to the bathroom to get ready for her day, whatever it was going to be. As she splashed cold water on her face and scrubbed off the last of the smeared makeup from her bimbo disguise, she vowed that if she survived this she would throw away all of her mascara once and for all.

Her toilet completed, she restlessly paced the room waiting to see if her captors would bring breakfast. She examined the windows again, but could see no way to work the bars loose. It was the same with the door lock. She was not going to get out of the room on her own.

Finally, she stopped pacing and sat on the edge of the bed. From her martial arts training, she knew that if she couldn't escape, she should conserve her energy. Lying back on the bed, she slowed her breathing and willed herself to relax. In minutes, she was asleep.

Sandra woke from her nap when she heard the familiar sound of helicopter rotors approaching the villa. For a moment she was disoriented and thought that she was back with Dragon Flight, but the stark reality of her true situation soon came crashing back around her.

She hurried to the window and saw the same blue and white Bell ship that had brought her here parked on the flat right outside the villa, its main rotor winding down. She also saw Miller, still in his Tac Force duty uniform, step out of the passenger side of the ship and head for the villa.

Her hands flew up to her face as she stepped back from the window. Her eyes frantically darted around the room to see if there was something she could use to defend herself. But there was nothing there she had not seen before.

She felt the panic rising and fought to hold it down. Sitting on the edge of the bed, she brought her breathing under control again. Miller was coming for her and there was not a thing she could do until he walked into the room. Maybe then she would have an opening. Until then, she could only wait and get ready.

CHAPTER 24

Tijuana, Mexico

The two guards led Gunner out of the Frienzia building to the small Bell chopper sitting on the landing pad. Sliding open the side door, they unceremoniously dumped him on the floor in the back and locked the door behind them.

The pilot was one of the blond, European types he had seen getting out of the Mangusta, and beside him sat one of the Mafia thugs. They both turned around to look at him and when they saw that he was helpless, they turned back and went about their business.

As soon as the chopper was in the air, Gunner started tugging against his bonds. The restraint was tight and the plastic band around his wrists cut into his flesh. From experience, he knew that he was not strong enough to break them and he gave up before he hurt himself.

Brute force was not going to free him, but he remembered hearing about a suspect who had been able to get his hands around in front of him while he was wearing the restraints. The guy had been limber enough to draw his feet up behind himself and slide his hands up over his feet. Gunner knew that he wasn't a contortionist, but it was the only chance he had.

For the first time in his life, Gunner appreciated being a

174

small man. Had he been as big and as muscular as either Wolff or Mojo, he would never have been able to even try to get his hands around in front of him. But, as skinny as he was, there was a slim chance that he might be able to do it.

Neither the European pilot nor the mafioso hood was paying any attention to him. They knew how tightly the plastic restraints around his wrists had been cinched down. There was no way that he was going to cause them any trouble.

Watching the back of the men's heads, Gunner levered the toe of one shoe against the heel of the other, and it popped off of his foot. It was more difficult to get the other one off, but somehow he managed that, too. Extending his arms as far as they would go, he drew his feet up tightly against his butt and tried to work his stockinged toes in between his ass and his bound wrists.

By pointing his toes until they cramped, he was able to get them wedged in under the restraint, but try as hard as he could, he couldn't get them worked in any further. The friction of his thick-issue cop socks kept his feet from sliding past his wrists. He would have to try to take them off, too.

It took longer for him to work the sweaty socks off his feet than it had his shoes. But he finally was able to work the toes of one foot into the top of his other sock and work it off. The second one went much more quickly, and once his feet were bare, he drew them up behind his back again.

This time, he was able to work the toes of both feet in between his butt and his wrists. Once they were firmly wedged in place, he pushed with all the strength in his legs. The sharp plastic band tore into his flesh, cutting through the skin and thin layers of muscle covering the wrist bones, as his feet inched their way past his wrists.

He bit his lip and continued to pull against the restraints as hard as he could while he punched. The blood from the cuts lubricated his skin and suddenly his bare feet slipped through.

He held his arms down where they were for a second,

letting the blood flow back into his hands as he studied the two men in the cockpit.

As he well knew, unlike the pilot of a fixed wing aircraft, a chopper pilot had to fly with both of his hands on the collective and cyclic controls at all times. Helicopters were inherently unstable and had to be flown every second that they were in the air. If the pilot took his hand off the controls even to scratch his ass, the chopper would start to go out of control. In reality, he could let go of the cyclic for an instant without anything drastic happening but not the spring-loaded collective. If he released it, the rotors dumped pitch and the chopper started falling out of the sky.

Even though the pilot was armed with an automatic pistol in a shoulder holster, he wouldn't be able to draw it and fire. Had he been armed with a double-action revolver, he could have drawn and fired it with one hand. But, unless the pilot already had a round chambered in the automatic and had it on safety, he would have to use both hands to draw the weapon and then pull back on the slide to chamber a round so he could fire.

And as Gunner knew, for safety reasons, an experienced pilot would never wear an automatic pistol with a round in the chamber.

That meant he should go for the guy in the passenger seat first.

The deck plates were slippery with his blood as he carefully got up to his knees. Once he had his balance, he lunged for the thug in the passenger seat, his arms held out in front of him. The thug caught the movement out of the corner of his eye, but before he could turn around, Gunner's arms were over his head and sliding down past his face.

"Hey!" the pilot yelled. "What..."

As soon as his hands were down past the thug's chin, Gunner hugged the back of the passenger seat as hard as he could, digging his bound wrists into the man's throat to cut off his breath.

The mafioso was caught between a rock and a hard place. If he used his hands to draw his pistol, Gunner would strangle him to death. But if he tried to keep Gunner from choking him, he couldn't shoot him.

The pilot took his hand from the cyclic to strike out at Gunner. But the hammering of the thug's feet against the rudder pedals made the chopper lurch in the air, and he grabbed for the controls again. He could only stare in horror at what was happening beside him.

The smart thing would have been for the mafioso to go for his pistol and shoot. But his survival instincts took over and his hands clawed frantically at the bound wrists choking the life out of him.

Gunner ignored the man's fingernails tearing at his wrists and pulled against his throat even harder. In seconds, the man's face grew red, his eyes bulged, and his feet beat a tattoo against the floor of the ship. The thug's hands suddenly went limp and fell to his side, but Gunner didn't relax his death grip for several more seconds.

And, when he did, his bound hands went for the pistol in the man's shoulder holster. "If you move," Gunner panted, the pistol raised to strike at the pilot, "I'll bust your fucking head open."

"Put it down, mister," the pilot said. "If you hit me we'll crash."

"No fuckin' way," Gunner grunted, his eyes narrowed. "I'll kill you first."

Something in Gunner's eyes convinced the pilot that he would do exactly that even if he died in the crash, too. "Okay," the pilot replied. "I will do what you want."

"Take your hand off the cyclic," Gunner said. "And open your side window. Then, carefully, real carefully, pull that pistol out of your holster and drop it out the window. You try anything smart, and I'll bash your fucking brains out."

The pilot did exactly as he was told.

"Now," Gunner said. "Keep both of your hands on those controls and don't move a muscle."

Holding his wrists up to his mouth, Gunner bit into the plastic restraints, his teeth tearing at his flesh at the same time. The plastic band was tough, but his teeth were sharp and it finally parted.

As soon as his hands were free, he racked back on the slide of the automatic to chamber a round. Holding the muzzle of the pistol against the side of the pilot's head, he reached across the body of the other man, and unfastened his seat belt. Then he reached out for the door lock on the passenger door and released it.

"Bank over to the right," he ordered the pilot, pressing the muzzle against his temple.

The pilot did as he was told, and when the passenger's body fell against the unlocked door, the door opened and he fell out. When the slipstream closed the door again, Gunner relocked it.

"Now," he said, moving the pistol away from the pilot's head. "Find a place to put this fucker down. Fast!"

Even though she was expecting it, Sandra was startled by the sound of the key in the door lock. Every nerve in her body went on full alert and she got to her feet. Miller had come back: to fulfill his threat.

Sandra had been a cop long enough to know when she was dealing with a psychotic personality, and there was no doubt in her mind that Miller was over the edge, completely over. She stood erect and controlled her panic, thinking that it might give her some psychological advantage if she didn't appear to fear him. Deep in her mind, however, she knew that no matter how unafraid she appeared, there was no way that she could escape this.

The door opened and he stood silently looking at her, his face obscured by the bright light pouring in from the hallway. He remained silent and, for a second, Sandra let herself believe that possibly some sense of reason had returned to him. This hope was shattered when he suddenly strode into the room, followed by two of the Mexican guards. The guards had nylon ropes in their hands.

"Tie her to the bed," he snapped, covering her with a large automatic pistol.

"You don't have to do this," she said evenly as the guards took her arms. "I'm no danger to you."

"No you're not," he smiled. "But that doesn't matter, does it? I owe you one and I'm going to see that you get it."

There was nothing Sandra could say in answer to that, so she allowed herself to be tied, spread-eagle, to the bed. Miller tested the bonds himself before dismissing the guards. As soon as the door shut behind them, he walked up to her and, hooking his hand in the top of her skimpy, see-through blouse, ripped it off her. For a second, he stared at her bared breasts, breathing harshly.

Slowly, his hands went down to the waistband of her miniskirt. With another sharp jerk, he snapped the button and zipper, tearing the thin fabric all the way to the hem. He whipped it away from her hips, his eyes fixed on her panties underneath. Those he slowly slipped down to mid-thigh before ripping them away.

He reached down and casually undid his belt, a slow grin spreading over his face again as he stared at her naked body. In one swift movement, he stepped up to her and the heavy military-style belt was flying through the air before she even had time to realize what was happening. She screamed as the heavy metal buckle cut across her breasts.

He jerked the belt back for another blow. "One more fucking sound out of you, bitch," he snarled, "and I'll cut them off. Got it? You've earned this, cunt, so just shut the fuck up and take it."

The belt came down again, even more savagely. She could feel blood flowing in the palms of her hands as her nails dug deeply into the soft flesh. She braced herself for the next blow. Her eyes were tightly shut, and she could hear his harsh breathing, but nothing happened. She looked up, a questioning look in her eyes.

He was staring at her breasts, breathing heavily, a glazed look in his eyes. She looked down to see bright red blood flowing from the deep cuts on both breasts. It covered her nipples and dripped down onto the bed.

The sight of her blood had inflamed him in a way that her naked, defenseless body had not. He fell upon her, his fists hammering at her, punching her torn breasts and stomach with repeated blows.

She tried to twist away from the savage assault, but there was no escape from his fists. A blow to the mouth smashed her lips against her teeth. Another one knocked the breath out of her. She clenched her teeth against the pain as she felt a darkness descending over her. She realized that she was close to passing out and welcomed the relief as she mercifully slipped into unconsciousness.

When Sandra's head slumped, Miller drew back from her. Fucking bitch! He hated fucking a dead body. She wasn't dead yet, but as far as he was concerned, she might as well be if she wasn't conscious and didn't know what was happening to her.

He briefly considered trying to bring her around. A lit cigarette properly applied to her nipples should snap her out of it fast enough. But maybe it would be better just to leave her alone for now. He smiled. This way when he came back, he could start all over from the beginning.

He ran the end of his duty belt back through the belt loops before buckling it. Bitch! When he was finished with her, she'd be sorry that she had passed out on him.

CHAPTER 25

Rio del Sangre, Mexico

As soon as the Bell chopper touched down on the empty desert floor, Gunner motioned toward the door with the pistol. "Out," he told the pilot.

"Do you want me to shut the turbine down?"

"No, just get out."

Leaving the turbine running at flight idle, the pilot carefully unbuckled his seat belt, opened the door, and stepped down onto the sand.

"Take three steps back," Gunner snapped. "Turn around and put your hands up in the air."

The pilot stood with his hands in the air as Gunner reached back in between the seats to recover his socks and shoes from the rear of the ship. As soon as he had them on again, he opened the first-aid kit mounted behind the pilot's seat, sprayed an antiseptic on his torn wrists, and bound them with gauze to stop the bleeding.

He found a package of Percodan, a heavy-duty pain pill, in the kit, but he decided against taking any of them; they might make him too fuzzy. The pain would give him the edge he would need to keep him alert for what he had to do in the next couple of hours.

"Okay," he said as he joined the pilot on the sand, the pistol aimed directly at his head. "Turn around and get down on your knees."

"Please, mister," the pilot pleaded as he knelt. "Please don't shoot me. I don't have anything to do with the business of those people, I just fly for them because they pay me well."

"Where are you from?"

"I am South African," the man said. "I was a pilot in the Air Force, but now I fly for money."

"And you don't care where your money comes from. Drugs, prostitution, murder."

"I don't know anything about that," the pilot said, his voice rising on the verge of panic. "They hired me just to fly their helicopters."

Gunner pulled the hammer of the pistol back. "Did you fly a tall blond woman somewhere for them recently?"

The pilot didn't hesitate for even a second. "Yes," he answered. "The day before yesterday."

"Where'd you take her?"

"To the Frienzia company villa at Rio del Sangre."

"Where the hell is that?"

"It's in a little town about twenty-three miles east of Tecate."

"Why did you take her there?"

"They told me to," he shrugged. "I heard that one of the gang wanted to see her."

"Who?"

"A man named Miller, that's all I know."

"Jim Miller? Tall, dark-haired, and always has a smart-ass smile on his face?"

"Yes," the pilot nodded. "That's the one, the police officer."

Gunner released the hammer. "You just earned yourself a chance to get out of this alive, buddy. All you have to do is to tell me exactly where this place is and what kind of landing control they use there."

"There's a map in the cockpit," the pilot said. "I can get it and show you where you have to go. And they do not have landing control. I radio ahead that I am coming and someone comes out to meet me."

"What's your call sign?"

"Tango Three Niner," the pilot said. "On two one six point five FM."

"Okay, buddy, on your feet. Get me the map, but I suggest that you move very carefully," Gunner cautioned, keeping the pistol on him. "You try anything cute and I'll fucking kill you."

Moving slowly, the pilot reached into the door pocket with shaking hands to retrieve his map. He opened it on the sand to show Gunner the villa and the surrounding area.

Gunner studied the map for a moment, but there was little to see. Just a villa and two big warehouses at the end of a dirt road on the outskirts of a small Mexican town in the middle of the desert.

"How many people are there?" Gunner asked. "And who are they?"

"Usually there are only the Mexican guards," the pilot replied. "Maybe a dozen of them, but sometimes some of the Frienzia people are there as well. They use the villa to have big parties and to entertain their guests. You know what I mean."

"Is that why you flew the woman there?"

The pilot looked down. "Yes."

"What kind of weapons do the guards have?"

"I have only seen pistols and some submachine guns carried by the guards."

Gunner folded the map. "Is there anything else I need to know about that place?"

The pilot thought for a moment. "The house is covered by

surveillance cameras and they usually keep the women in a small room on the ground floor."

"Okay, buddy." Gunner brought the pistol up again. "On your feet, turn around and start running."

The pilot looked panicked. "But there's nothing out here. I'll die of thirst."

"Not if I put a bullet through your fucking head," Gunner said as he thumbed the hammer back. The click of the hammer going back echoed off the side of the chopper.

The pilot spun around and took off like a shot, running halfway hunched over as if expecting a shot in the back at any moment.

The pilot was still running across the open desert when Gunner strapped himself into the pilot's seat. Running the turbine back up to full RPM, he pulled pitch on the collective and the small ship lifted off the desert floor and banked away to the north. As soon as he reached cruising altitude, he switched the radio over to the Dragon Flight emergency frequency and started transmitting.

Sandra was startled out of her light, restless sleep by the sound of a key being inserted into the lock of her cell. Her battered body ached and she was beyond exhaustion, but her body went on full alert at the sound. She struggled against her bonds, trying to sit up, but she knew there was no way that she could escape this.

The door opened and Miller quickly strode into the room shutting the door behind him. He walked up to her without saying a word, a smile firmly in place on his face. His hand slowly came down to touch the bruised and cut fresh of her breasts like a lover's caress.

She cringed as his fingers traced the belt cuts across her breasts and belly and slowly wiped across the still wet rivulets of blood oozing from her wounds. The look of lust that sprang into his eyes was so frightening that she had to turn her face away.

He saw the movement and whipped his hand across her face, breaking open her split lip. "Don't turn your face away from me, bitch," he snapped, his hands going to his belt buckle. "Or do you want more of this?"

She shook her head, but he unbuckled the belt and pulled it from the loops anyway. Instead of striking her with it, however, he slowly lowered the buckle down onto her flesh. She flinched from the contact and he laughed. "What's the matter," he asked. "A tough broad like you shouldn't be afraid of a belt. You aren't afraid of it, are you?"

She didn't know if it was better for her to admit her fear or not, so she nodded her head.

"You are? Good." He snapped the belt back and in one swift movement, the heavy military-style belt was flying through the air before she even had time to realize what was happening. She screamed as the heavy metal buckle cut into the skin of her belly above her pubic hair. The belt snapped back and flashed down again striking in the same place. She could feel blood trickling across her skin as she tensed herself for another blow, but it did not come.

He was standing in between her bound ankles staring at her belly, his breath coming in harsh, uneven gasps, The sight of her fresh blood was inflaming him again. He dropped the belt and without taking his eyes from her, he quickly undid his pants and kicked them off. She stared numbly at his erect penis as he climbed up on to the end of the bed and knelt in between her outstretched thighs. This could not be happening to her.

She twisted her head from side to side, moaning with fear. She knew that pleas were useless.

Suddenly he was on top of her, his weight momentarily knocking the air out of her lungs. He reached down in between her legs and, with one quick lunge, drove himself partway up inside her.

Her scream sounded like that of a dying animal as he tore his way deeper into her. She was not lubricated, and her fear had caused her vaginal muscles to tighten even more. The pain was excruciating, unbearable. It felt as if he was ripping her open.

Miller seemed oblivious to her now as he started ramming himself deeper and deeper into her, his head turned to one side and his eyes tightly closed. His hands reached up and he dug his fingers deeply into the bruised flesh of her wounded breasts.

She bit back another scream of pain and turned her head away, closing her eyes. She tried with every ounce of strength she had left to distance herself from what was happening to her body, but she could not escape the feeling of his body invading hers.

Her vagina burned as his penis thrust again and again into her unwilling softness. His breathing had turned into a panting, hitching sound as he hammered his way toward his climax. He turned his head back to hers and buried his face in her hair.

She shuddered at this gesture, somehow more intimate than his violation of her and twisted her face as far away from him as she could.

His thrusts became deeper and faster as he slammed his body against hers as if trying to penetrate some invisible wall. Her entire pelvic area felt as if it were on fire, and suddenly something deep inside her gave way. Her screams reverberated down the long hallway.

The men Miller had left on guard outside the door exchanged uneasy glances. One of them quickly crossed himself. The blond woman sounded like an animal being slaughtered, but they knew better than to try to do anything about it. Señor Miller was a bad hombre to cross, particularly when he was in there with one of his women. They could only ignore the screams.

The screams cut off abruptly, however, as Sandra slipped

back into unconsciousness again.

Miller stopped abruptly and raised himself off her body. Fucking bitch, she had done it again and he felt himself starting to go soft. What did he have to do to keep her awake? It just wasn't the same if she wasn't awake and couldn't appreciate what he was doing to her. He pulled out of her, climbed down off of the bed, and reached for his pants on the floor.

She had foiled him again, but if she thought that she was going to escape her punishment by passing out every time things really got going, she was badly mistaken. The next time he came in to visit her, he would bring the high-voltage generator they used when they needed to talk to a street dealer who had been late with his payment.

He chuckled to himself when he thought of wiring her nipples for half a million volts. He was sure that he could keep her awake with that. But if it didn't, no problem, he'd simply turn up the amperage on the generator and burn her tits off. That could also be interesting, too, he realized as he felt himself grow hard again. Maybe he'd do that first the next time as a way to warm her up so she'd appreciate him more.

The men in the hallway turned their eyes away as Miller stepped out of the room and locked the door behind him.

Gunner's call electrified the small Dragon Flight CP. As soon as Gunner identified himself, Mom stabbed the panic button on her console that activated the remote speakers in Buzz's office. When he heard Gunner's voice, Buzz came out of his chair as if he had been shot and raced around the corner into the commo center.

As Gunner tersely reported the situation in Mexico, Buzz charted the location of both the villa and the Frienzia manufacturing plant on the big map on the wall. When Gunner finished his report and said that he was going in after Sandra,

Buzz reached for the radio mike. "Gunner, this is Command One, come in."

There was no answer, only static on the Dragon Flight emergency frequency.

"Gunner, this is Buzz!" he shouted over the dead radio. "Answer me, damnit! Wait till I can get some forces in there to help you."

When there was no response, he turned to Ruby. "Quick," he said. "Put me through to Wolff!"

Wolff and Mugabe were cruising through the smog over LA when Mom's voice came in over their head phones. "Dragon One Zero, this is Dragon Control."

"One Zero, go ahead."

"This is Control, switch to Scramcom One."

Wolff looked over to Mojo with a question on his face as he switched the radio over to the scrambled communications system. Scramcom was only used when things were getting serious and it was about fucking time. "One Zero on Scramcom One, go."

"This is Command One," came Buzz's voice over the headset. "We have just received a radio call from Officer Jennings. He says that he is in Mexico and he has just escaped from the drug gang responsible for the Mangusta robberies. They are also holding Officer Revell hostage and he is en route to her location now to attempt to free her."

Wolff and Mugabe exchanged startled glances. Legs was being held captive?

"Dragon One Four is being scrambled right now with a Tac team and a medic in the back. He is to form up with you and you will fly to Gunner's location Code Zero."

"One Zero, copy," Wolff answered. "Send the location."

Buzz quickly gave Wolff the coordinates for Rio del Sangre. "I'll contact the Mexican authorities and have flight clearance by the time you reach the border."

Wolff keyed his mike as he twisted the throttle open to maximum RPM. "Good copy, we're on our way."

CHAPTER 26

High over Mexico

As soon as his call to Dragon Flight was completed, Gunner switched his radio over to the drug gang's radio frequency. Even if Buzz could get his forces assembled immediately and got permission from the Mexican government to cross the border, he knew that it would be hours before anyone could get in to free Sandra. And, if Miller was there with her like the pilot had said, he couldn't let her stay in his hands a minute longer than was absolutely necessary.

Banking the chopper over, he twisted the throttle all the way up against the stop as he took up a course heading for the villa at Rio del Sangre.

He monitored the gang's radio frequency on the flight in. He had no intention of radioing ahead to let them know that he was coming, but he needed to know if they spotted him on the way in and were trying to contact him.

As he approached the small town, he spotted the warehouses and villa in a valley on the north side of the village. The place appeared to be deserted, but he took no chances. Dropping down low, he brought the blue-and-white Bell chopper in for a fast landing on the concrete pad alongside the biggest of the two warehouses. He had lucked out; no one was waiting there to meet him.

Thumbing back the hammer on his pistol, he opened the door of the chopper and stepped down onto the hard-packed earth of the landing pad. He waited for a moment to make sure that he was alone before sprinting for the side of the warehouse. Once under cover, he looked back at the villa some two hundred meters away.

He needed something to use as a diversion to draw attention away from the villa so he could get there without being spotted. A fire was always a good diversion and he decided to slip into the warehouse to see if he could find something to burn.

Looking around the corner of the side of the building, he saw a door covered by a wide-angle lens security camera. He watched the camera for a moment and saw that it tracked from left to right covering the approaches to the door. Timing the sweep, he found that he would only have a little less than a minute to reach the door from the time the camera turned away until it turned back again and would pick him up.

Gathering his feet under himself, he leaped up and raced for the door. It was unlocked so he carefully opened it and slipped into the dark warehouse. When he paused to allow his eyes to adjust to the darkness, he saw that he was surrounded by stacks of fifty-five gallon drums. Most of the drums bore flammable material warning labels.

The faint sound of laughter from a television set caught his ears. Someone was in the warehouse. Silently making his way around the stacks of drums, he reached an aisle and looked across the warehouse. Against the opposite wall was a small table with a bank of security camera monitors mounted above it. Under the monitors was a small TV set tuned to what looked like a *Love Boat* rerun.

No one was at the table and, keeping well out of sight, Gunner looked around to see where the guard was. Just then, a Mexican wearing a khaki shirt and blue jeans stepped out from behind a partition at the other end of the wall from the table, probably the latrine.

The guard slowly walked back to the table, sat down again, and turned up the volume on the TV set. Gunner waited until the guard settled down with his feet up on the table before silently leaving his hiding place. A few swift steps put him within striking range and he lashed out with the gun barrel, smashing it into the side of the guard's head right behind his ear. The guard fell sideways out of his chair and hit the floor with a heavy thud.

Gunner stepped past him and turned the TV set down. Noticing the pile of cigarette butts in the ash tray, he went through the unconscious guard's pockets looking for a cigarette lighter and found it in his right front shirt pocket. Gathering up the guard's pile of skin magazines, he went back to the stacks of drums. From the labels on the containers he had seen, the warehouse would go up like a big bomb once a fire got going.

Tearing pages from the magazines, he crumpled the paper and stuffed it under the wooden pallet under a stack of drums. Seeing several empty pallets nearby, he broke them up and added the wood to his pile before looking around for even more fuel. The other side of the building looked like it was used for vehicle maintenance, and when he walked over to investigate it, he found several quarts of motor oil and a gas can.

Pouring the oil down the side of the bottom drum, he laid down a trail of gasoline back toward the front door. Flicking the lighter to life, he ignited the gas trail and watched it race back to the stack of drums. The paper ignited instantly and started the wooden pallet ablaze. In seconds, the flames were licking up the sides of the drums and it was time for him to go.

The fire and resulting explosions were bound to bring someone from town to investigate, the local police or the fire department, and he didn't want anyone to get in the way of what he had to do.

That fucker Miller was his. All his.

Keeping to what little cover there was, he sprinted across the open ground for the main house. The rear gate in the security fence around the villa was fitted with an electronic lock and was covered by another surveillance camera. Gunner couldn't waste the time to find a way to get around the camera now—the drums would go up at any second. Resting his wrists against the top of the fence to steady the pistol he shot out the camera. Another shot opened the gate and he crashed through it, sprinting for the back side of the villa.

At any moment, he expected to see armed guards come rushing out of the villa toward him, but he made it safely to the vestibule over the back door. Though he was apparently still unseen, he knew that it was only a matter of seconds at the most before someone came to investigate the shots.

Trying the doorknob, he found it unlocked and, carefully opening the door, slipped inside the villa. As his eyes adjusted to the dim light inside, he found himself in a long hallway with several doors off both sides. Holding the pistol in a ready position, he started down the hall when a faint sound of whimpering coming from behind the first door stopped him cold. It sounded like a woman in pain.

He tried the handle and it was locked. "Sandra?" he whispered as loud as he dared. "It's me, Gunner."

Putting his ear to the door, he thought he heard Sandra call his name. Drawing his leg up, he kicked flat-footed at the door plate, throwing his weight against it. The lock gave way and the door slammed open throwing him off balance as he fell into the darkened room.

"Gunner?" came the voice from the other end of the room.

"Sandra? It's me."

"Oh, God," she sobbed. "Gunner."

His eyes adjusted to the darkness in the room and he saw Sandra lying on the top of the bed, her arms and legs spread out. As he rushed to her side and started tearing at the ropes that bound her, he tried not to look at her nakedness, but he could not help but see the blood shining black in the light from the hallway.

"Who did this to you?"

Sandra choked back a sob. "Miller," she said softly, her voice so low that he could hardly hear her. "Jim Miller. He's working with the drug gang. He beat me and..." Her voice broke. "And he... he..."

Impulsively, he took her in his arms, cradling her head against his shoulder. He was very aware of her nakedness, but it made him feel even more protective of her. His free hand caressed her hair like he was calming a frightened child as sobs wracked her body.

When he heard a noise from the floor above, he released her and handed her the pistol. "Here," he said. "Take this. You'll be safe till I get back."

"Be careful, please be careful," she whispered, her voice breaking. "He's...he's..." she sobbed, unable to continue.

"It's okay," he said through clenched teeth. "Don't worry, I'll take care of him."

As he pulled the door shut behind him, he heard the sound of gunfire coming from the direction of the warehouses. If the Tac teams were on the ground, it wouldn't be long before they started their assault on the villa.

No matter what else happened here today, he had to get to Miller before they did. This was one score that he had to settle for himself. He had warned Miller what would happen to him if he hurt Sandra, and Gunner Jennings was a man who always kept his promises.

Back out in the hallway, Gunner frantically looked for

something to use as a weapon. Leaving his pistol with Sandra had left him unarmed, but she needed it more than he did right now.

Hanging on the wall at the end of the hall was one of those decorative plaques that one saw for sale in every Mexican tourist-trap border-town bazaar. The red velvet plaque mounted a pair of bullfighters' daggers behind a phony crest of arms beaten into a tin shield. He knew that the daggers' blades would be shit, melted down beer cans more than likely, but they were weapons.

He pulled the daggers from the plaque, and, sticking one of them in his belt, tested the blade of the other. As he had thought, the blade had a rounded cutting edge and absolutely no temper to the metal at all. But at least he could stab with it and hope that the blade didn't bend as it went in.

Just then he heard a noise from the top of the stairs to his right. Without waiting to see who it was, he dashed up the stairs, the dagger held ready in his right hand.

A Mexican guard was on the top of the stairs, half turned back as if he were looking at someone in the upper room. He saw Gunner only in time to take the dagger blade into his side, below the ribs. The blade deflected a little, but it pierced the man's shirt. Gunner felt it slide through the thin layer of muscles and drive on into his guts. He gave the dagger a vicious twist and, feeling the blade bend inside the man's body, released it and stepped back.

The Mexican screamed as he fell back against the wall, clutching his abdomen. Gunner snatched the other dagger from his belt and thrust the point of the blade into his throat, cutting off his scream. The man crumpled on the stairs at his feet.

The Mexican had a broad-bladed Bowie knife in a sheath on his belt. Gunner dropped the cheap dagger and leaned down to draw the Bowie. Now he was ready to meet Miller. Standing up, he cautiously peered around the corner at the top of the stairs.

The shot came with no warning.

Gunner staggered back from the blow to his upper left arm. A second shot slammed into the wall by his chest. "Miller!" he screamed. "I'm coming to kill you!"

He crouched on the stairs as Miller fired again and again. The pistol rounds sang past his head and smashed into the stairs, but the heavy wooden steps protected him. When he heard Millets pistol click on an empty magazine, he stood up. Stepping out around the landing, he faced Miller, his left arm hanging limply at his side, but the Bowie knife was in his right hand. He was running on pure adrenaline that blocked the pain of his wound. His face wore a terrible expression and his lips were drawn back, baring his teeth.

"You're mine now, you bastard." Gunner smiled a terrible smile. "And I'm going to cut your balls off, just like I promised you I would."

Miller's eyes darted all around the room, but there was nowhere he could run. The stairs were to Gunner's back. He threw the empty pistol at Gunner's head, but the pilot merely moved aside to let it pass harmlessly by him.

"Jennings!" Miller called out, a note of panic in his voice. "You're a cop! You can't do this! You have to arrest me!"

"Wrong again," Gunner smiled. "I'm not a cop, you saw to that. I resigned from the force when you shit on Sandra. A cop would arrest you, but I'm going to kill you."

A panicked Miller rushed at him, but Gunner, slashing out with the knife, quickly stepped back. The Bowie's blade laid Miller's face open to the bone. He screamed and fell back, his hands going up to his face. Gunner stepped in close to him again, the Bowie slashing like a striking snake. This time the blade flashed across his upper right arm, slashing through the muscles. As Miller reached for his wounded arm with his left hand, Gunner lashed out savagely again, laying his other arm open from the elbow to the wrist.

Miller screamed shrilly and staggered backward, now

trying to staunch the blood flowing freely from both his arms. His face lost all of its humanity. There was nothing in his eyes but sheer animal terror.

There was nothing in Gunner's face as he stalked Miller but a fierce killing lust.

When Miller's retreat was stopped by the far wall, Gunner quickly closed the gap between them. Stepping up to the cowering Miller, he slowly thrust the knife into his upper belly, right below the breastbone. He felt the momentary resistance as the heavy blade pierced each of the layers of skin and muscle.

Miller's crazed eyes followed the knife as it gutted him, his mouth open in a soundless scream.

When the hilt of the Bowie was pressed tightly against Miller's skin, Gunner withdrew the knife until only a few inches of the blade were still in him. Taking a deep breath, he ripped the knife down through Miller's belly until it was stopped by the renegade cop's belt buckle.

Miller's high-pitched scream echoed in the room as his gut spilled out of his split abdominal cavity. His bladder emptied at the same time, adding the rank smell of urine to the overpowering stench of fear, fresh blood, and punctured intestines.

Gunner stepped back as Miller went down to his knees, vainly trying to stuff his wet guts back into his body. His eyes frantically darted from side to side as if he were looking for help or even mercy.

But there was no mercy in Gunner's face. Nor was there any help for him anywhere in the hacienda.

"Please," he whispered.

"Die!" Gunner snarled. "You miserable son of a bitch. Die!"

Miller staggered to his feet, his hands cradling his slippery, looped intestines. "Please?"

Gunner started for him again, the knife held low. "Now,"

he said softly, "I'm going to cut your nuts off, just like I said I would."

Miller spun around and stumbled for the window behind him. "No!" he screamed. "Please!"

"Fuck you!"

"Nooooo!"

Miller threw himself against the glass to escape the knife. It shattered under the impact, sending him hurtling down onto the wrought-iron spikes of the security fence below. His screams cut off abruptly when one of the spikes pierced his throat. His feet kicking in the air, he bled to death in seconds.

CHAPTER 27

The California-Mexico Border

As Wolff approached the Mexican border at full throttle, he didn't want to have to wait to have to get clearance from Buzz, but he knew that he had to check in with Dragon Control. He could bullshit his way through things like air-traffic control regulations when he was in the States, but unless he wanted a Mexican Air Force F-16 Falcon sending a missile up his ass, he had better play it safe and follow by the rules this time. "Dragon Control, this is One Zero," he radioed.

"Request flight clearance for Mexico."

"This is Control, wait one."

"Damnit, Control!" he snapped back. "I'm at the border now and Legs is waiting. Get me my clearance now, or I'll go in without it."

"One Zero, this is Command One" came Buzz's controlled voice over his headset a second later. "You are clear to enter Mexico airspace for a course heading to Rio del Sangre. Be advised that a force of Mexican drug police agents along with a contingent of American DEA observers are already at the scene, so stay alert for possible Federale choppers operating in the area."

"Copy," Wolff replied. "Do you have an attack map overlay for the area?"

"That's affirm," Buzz answered. "Go to Tac Link for download."

Mojo quickly established the computer link between their speeding gunship and the Dragon Flight command post back in LA. "Command, this is One Zero X Ray," he radioed. "Tac Link is established, go ahead."

In seconds, all of the information Mom had been able to gather on the Rio del Sangre location and the gang's Frienzia drug-manufacturing plant was sent to the chopper's computer at the speed of light. Mojo's tactical screen came alive with the data.

"This is One Zero X Ray, Tac Link completed."

"Command One copy," Buzz replied. "Negative further at this time, keep me informed."

"One Zero, clear."

Gunner looked down from the shattered second story window of the villa. When he saw that Miller was dead, he was greatly disappointed.

It had gone much too fast. He should have hamstrung the bastard so he couldn't have jumped before he had time to castrate him. It was too late now, but at least the motherfucker was dead. Wiping the knife blade clean on a piece of torn curtain, he put it back in his belt. Looking over toward the blazing warehouse, he saw a Mexican Federal Tac team dressed in tan-and-brown desert camouflage uniforms approaching the villa using fire and movement. Help had finally arrived, but apparently some of the gang's guards were fighting back. He had to stop the police assault before they fired on the villa and endangered Sandra.

He rushed back down the stairs, pausing briefly at the door to Sandra's room. He heard nothing and continued on. He would have time to go back to her as soon as he notified the Federalies that she was there.

Dashing out the back door, he took cover behind the wall at the back gate. The Mexican Tac team spotted him and a burst of fire chipped brick splinters from the side of the ornamental gate.

"Don't shoot!" he shouted, holding his arms high in the air. "I'm a cop!"

The firing stopped and a voice called out in English for him to stay where he was and to keep his hands in sight. While the one Mexican Tac cop held him in his sights, another one stepped out and walked up to him, a 7.62mm H and K assault rifle leveled on him. As he approached, Gunner saw that the man was wearing an American DEA patch on the breast of his desert camouflage uniform.

"Who are you?" The muzzle of the cop's assault rifle didn't waver an inch; neither did Gunner's hands. "I'm Flight Sergeant Gunner Jennings of the Tac Force."

"What in the hell is a chopper cop doing down here in Mexico?"

"I could ask you the same thing," Gunner answered. "But I'm on an undercover assignment out of Torrance Airfield in LA."

"You have any ID?"

Gunner shook his head. "I told you I'm undercover, I'm clean. Call the Tac Force, they can vouch for me."

The Tac cop kept Gunner covered as he spoke into his throat mike. After a minute, he released his mike button. "Do you go by the name of Gunner?"

Gunner nodded.

The rifle came down. "You've got one of your buddies inbound in just a few minutes. A Dragon One Zero with someone named the Wolfman on board."

For the first time in days, Gunner allowed a slow smile to pass over his face. Wolff and Mugabe were coming, and that meant that this nightmare was finally over. As relief came over him and the adrenaline was scrubbed from his bloodstream, he finally started to feel the effects of his wound. His face went white and he squeezed his eyes shut as a wave of pain swept over him.

The DEA Tac Cop turned around and shouted something in Spanish. "I called for my medic," he explained, "You need to have that wound looked after."

"Not me." Gunner gritted his teeth as he shook his head. "There's another officer back in the villa and she's hurt pretty bad."

"What happened to her?"

"One of these bastards beat and raped her."

"We have an ambulance and a doctor standing by," the Tac Cop said, clicking in his throat mike. "They'll be here in a minute."

As soon as the medics arrived, Gunner led them in to Sandra. Now he could tell her that everything was okay. He knew that nothing would ever really be okay for her again. But he thought that maybe she would stop crying if he told her that Miller couldn't hurt her anymore.

As he approached Rio del Sangre, Wolff made contact with the Mexican forces on the ground before even trying to land. Even though the Griffin prominently displayed the Tac Force markings, he knew that there had been some kind of firefight down there and he didn't want to risk itchy trigger fingers. He was quickly patched through to the DEA agent with the Mexicans and received permission to land.

The DEA agent was waiting to meet him when he stepped down from the Griffin. "Where's our people?" Wolff asked.

The agent pointed over to the ambulance where a medic was bandaging a man's shoulder. It was Gunner.

"Gunner," Wolff said, walking up to him. "Where's Legs?"

Gunner looked back into the vehicle where a Mexican medic was administering a bottle of IV blood expander to her. Another one was holding an oxygen mask to her face.

"What happened?"

"Miller," Gunner answered his voice flat and expressionless.

"Miller?" Wolff frowned. "What do you mean?"

"He was working with the gang," Gunner said, his voice grim. "He beat her up pretty badly and then raped her."

Wolff's face went hard. "Where is he?"

"Under the blanket," Gunner said, pointing to the still form with the blanket over his head. "I killed him with a knife."

Wolff walked over and lifted the blanket from Miller's body. One quick glance was enough for him and he quickly lowered it again. Miller looked like he had stepped into a buzz saw. Gunner had done more than just kill him; he had butchered him. Wolff felt no pity for the renegade cop, however. If he had laid even a hand on Sandra, he deserved everything he had received and more. Wolff had to resist the urge to kick the body for good measure.

When Wolff returned, Mojo called out that Knox and Gordon were inbound in Dragon One Four and could medevac Legs and Gunner back to LA. As soon as the chopper landed, Wolff helped the medics load Sandra's litter into the back of One Four. After seeing that she was strapped down and was as comfortable as he could make her, Wolff went back to get Gunner. But, as he was walking the wounded man to the ship, the DEA agent came up to them.

"I'm afraid that Gunner's going to have to stay here with me and the authorities," he said. "Until we can get this mess straightened out."

Although he didn't want to leave Gunner behind, Wolff

knew better than to make an issue of it. After all, Gunner wasn't a Tac Force officer anymore; now he was a murder suspect.

"It's okay," Gunner told Wolff. "You just make sure that Sandra gets back safely."

"Keep an eye on him for me, will you?" Wolff asked the drug cop.

"Sure thing."

As soon as Wolff was airborne with One Four flying alongside, he set a course directly back to LA and got on the radio to make a full report on the shootout at Rio del Sangre. Buzz acknowledged the report and gave orders for him to break away and head over to Tijuana to reinforce the Tac team going in to capture the Frienzia facility. Specifically, he was to fly air cover for the Griffins carrying the Tac teams in case the two Mangustas tried to interfere with the operation.

That suited Wolff to a T. Even with all that had gone down in the last week, he still hadn't forgotten that he owed those bastards for the damage they had done to his Corsair in Reno. He was more than happy to go hunting with his Griffin.

Getting extended flight clearance for Mexican airspace, he banked away from One Four and set a course to the west flying down the California-Mexican border.

A few minutes later, Mom's urgent voice came in over Wolff's helmet earphones. "Dragon One Zero," she radioed. "This is Dragon Control."

He clicked in his throat mike. "One Zero, go."

"This is Control," Mom answered. "We have a report that the two Mangusta gunships have escaped from the Frienzia drug lab and are headed east toward your location with two Griffins in pursuit."

A broad smile spread over Wolff's face. He didn't have to hunt the Mangustas down after all; they were coming to him.

205

"Good copy, Control," he answered. "I'll see if I can get the boys to vector them in to me so Mojo and I can arrange a little surprise for them."

"Control, copy," Mom replied. "Command One advises that you have tactical control."

"One Zero, copy."

"Control, clear."

Wolff grinned broadly. It was about time that Buzz gave him something to do. And if the Mangustas thought that they were going to pull that stealth chopper shit getaway this time, they were sadly mistaken.

In the left-hand seat, Mugabe got ready to go to war. He activated his acquisition radar and armed the weapons in the nose turret. He dialed in a mix of armor-piercing and high-explosive ammunition for the 25mm chain gun and a straight load of HE rounds for the 40mm grenade launcher. When they caught up with the Mangustas, he was simply going to blow their sorry asses out of the air, no questions asked. And, no warnings given, either.

Wolff switched over to the Griffin frequency and clicked in his throat mike. "Dragon One Two and One Three, this is Dragon One Zero. Be advised that I am now Dragon Lead, standby for Tac Link hookup. I've got a plan."

CHAPTER 28

High Above the Mexican Border

Wolff's aerial ambush worked perfectly. The other two pursuing Griffins had kept to the south of the fleeing Mangustas preventing them from turning and going deeper into Mexico. Wolff had ordered them to keep up with the two gunships at any cost and they had been running on over-rev since leaving T Town. They were drinking a lot of fuel, but they had done their job.

Wolff was waiting for the Mangustas when they appeared. And he made sure that they knew he was there.

As soon as the Tac link with the other Griffins showed them to be only a couple of miles away, Mugabe switched on his targeting radar and locked it on the two gunships, With the old radar system he would only have been able to track one of the targets, but the new sets Red had installed allowed him to lock on to both of them at the same time.

When the radar lock-on warning alarms sounded in the cockpits of the Mangustas, their pilots started taking evasive action. This slowed their headlong flight and allowed the trailing Griffins to get right on their tails.

As Wolff closed in on the gunships from the front and closed the trap, he switched his radio to the international air emergency frequency. "Mangusta choppers," he radioed. "This is the United States Tactical Police Force. Slow your aircraft to one hundred knots and take up a heading of three zero zero degrees. We will escort you back to Los Angeles."

With Wolff in front of them and the Griffins blocking their retreat into southern Mexico, the two Mangustas whirled around in the sky and fled to the north, back into the United States. That was what Wolff had wanted, now that he had them back on his own turf. They would either give up peacefully or he would blow them out of the sky. He hoped, however, that they would put up a fight. He wanted to show them what he could do when he had live ammunition on board.

Wolff keyed his mike as he dove after them to take up the pursuit. "Control, this is One Zero, be advised that the two bandits are heading into US airspace, One Three and I are in hot pursuit, inform air traffic control."

"Control copy," Mom replied. "Do you want Air Defense Command assistance?"

"That's a negative," Wolff almost shouted. "We don't need jets, we have them cornered."

"Control copy. Command One says that he is alerting the California State Patrol chopper units and they'll be standing by if you need them."

"One Zero, copy," Wolff answered. "Tell them they can help us by keeping them away from the cities."

"Control, clear."

"We're losing them," Mojo said, his eyes watching the tactical radar readout. The Mangustas were steadily pulling away as they headed up through the desert to the east of San Diego.

Wolff twisted the throttle even harder up against the stop, but his airspeed didn't change. It was time to go to over-rev. The Griffin's twin GE T-700 turbines drank JP-4 jet fuel at a frightening rate on over-rev, and if he stayed in it too long, it would scrap the turbines, but he had no choice—he couldn't let them get away now. If Wolff could keep the gunships from dropping down low and losing themselves in the built-up areas, they would either have to give up or turn and fight sooner or later.

His hand reached out and, flipping the over-rev control switch, sent the turbines screaming. His airspeed promptly climbed and, keeping his eyes on the Mangusta's radar blip, he followed after them.

"You're closing the gap," Mojo reported a few minutes later. "But we're losing One Three. He's low on fuel and can't keep up."

"Give him our heading," Wolff replied. "And tell him to stay with us as long as he can." By now, the choppers were well past the San Diego area and were closing in on Anaheim on the southern outskirts of greater Los Angeles.

"I've got them in sight," Wolff confirmed as his hand switched the turbines out of over-rev. The Mangustas seemed to have slowed down; maybe they too were worried about conserving fuel. Suddenly, the trailing Mangusta whirled around in the sky and climbed up into an attack position.

"We've got lock-on!" Mojo shouted, his finger poised above the decoy flare-launching button.

"I've got him!" Wolff stomped down on the right rudder pedal to bring the ship around to face the Mangusta and to hide the telltale exhausts of his turbines from the deadly air-to-air missiles. Even with the decoy flares, he was vulnerable if the renegade gunship fired a heat-seeking missile.

"It's only gun radar," Mojo reported. "He's not carrying missiles."

Wolff smiled. That was more like it. Now they could do this thing the old-fashioned way, a gun-to-gun shootout in the sky. He hauled up on the collective to pull pitch to the rotor blades as he twisted in full throttle and nudged forward on the cyclic control. Tail high, the Griffin rose to meet the Mangusta.

For a moment, the two gunships maneuvered against each other, their guns silent, looking for a favorable attack position. Suddenly, the Mangusta banked over sharply, dropped her nose to line up with the Griffin, and opened fire.

Wolff had been expecting his opponent to try something like that, and he was ready for it. The instant that the Mangusta kicked her tail around, he chopped his pitch and shoved the Griffin's nose down. The Mangusta's gun turret could traverse from side to side, but could not elevate far enough down to hit a target diving beneath her.

The burst of 20mm fire passed harmlessly over the top of the diving Griffin. Now it was Wolff's turn.

As the Mangusta flashed past overhead, Wolff kicked down on his right rudder pedal, slammed the cyclic over to the right-hand corner, and pulled maximum pitch to the rotor blades. With the turbine still delivering full RPM, the chopper heeled over onto her right side as the blades clawed the air. The massive torque of the forty-foot rotor spun the ship around on its axis. Applying left pedal and shoving forward on the cyclic, Wolff brought his ship around behind the Mangusta and gave Mojo a fleeting shot.

The gunner's fingers tightened on the firing controls as he walked his 25mm fire into the tail boom of the Mangusta. A bright blossom of fire appeared in front of the tail rotor and the gunship slowly began to twist around to the right. Another burst of fire cut into the main rotor masthead smashing the cyclic control system.

With his tail rotor and cyclic controls shot out, it was all that the Mangusta's pilot could do to keep his machine in the air. Mojo held his fire as Wolff flew in closer behind the gunship. Wolff was keying his mike to order the pilot to surrender when the Mangusta suddenly nosed over into a dive and headed straight for the crowded freeway below.

Slamming his throttle forward, Wolff banked over to the

left and dove down after the Mangusta in a vain try to warn the drivers on the highway below, but the Mangusta was flying too fast for him to catch up with it.

The diving gunship slammed straight into the bridge abutment and disappeared into a huge, boiling ball of flame. Flaming debris showered down onto the freeway scattering the cars as they swerved to avoid it. Several cars collided or skidded to a halt in the emergency lanes, but none of them seemed to have gotten caught up in the explosion. The civilian casualties shouldn't be too great.

Wolff pulled up and quickly reported the crash to Control, requesting that the local police and ambulances be dispatched ASAP. As soon as Mom acknowledged his message, he climbed back up and headed north again. "Where'd that other bastard go?" he asked Mojo.

The gunner flashed the long-range radar plot over to the pilot's HUD screen. The blip showed that the other gunship was still fleeing north as fast as it could go. In a few more minutes, it would be on the northern outskirts of LA.

"Let's get him," Wolff said as he hit the over-rev switch again. The last gunship had a head start on him, but maybe he could convince the pilot to slow down so they could play. He switched the radio over to the international emergency frequency again and keyed his throat mike.

"Mangusta chopper," he radioed. "This is the Wolfman in the Tac Force Griffin coming up behind you. I just nailed your little buddy. He's splattered all over the freeway. You were pretty good at shooting down unarmed aircraft and armored cars in Reno, asshole, but how'd you like to try your luck against someone who can shoot back?"

When the Mangusta didn't respond, Wolff keyed his mike again. "I'm not going to let you get away, asshole, so you might as well either give it up or turn around and face me. Either way, motherfucker, your ass is mine."

The HUD display showed the Mangusta's blip slowing down as the gunship turned around in the sky. Wolff grinned broadly. "Okay," he said. "Here we go."

The two gunships approached each other at over three hundred miles an hour. Before they got within gun range, however, the Mangusta pulled into a sharp banking turn, the classic opening move for a dog fight.

"Okay motherfucker," Wolff grunted with the G force as he threw his ship into an opposing turn. "Let's see just how fucking good you really are."

Both ships fought for altitude as they circled. In a dogfight, the ship with the altitude advantage also had the tactical advantage, and both pilots knew this. Even though he was running low on fuel, Wolff kept both his turbines screaming at 100 percent RPM. This was not the time to be worried about fuel conservation.

So far, neither pilot had been able to find an opening that would let them take a shot without exposing themselves to return fire. Tired of flying circles in the sky, Wolff gambled. Making a hard bank, he turned into the Mangusta's guns. In the split second before the gunship could open fire, however, Wolff stood his Griffin up on his side, giving Mojo an opening to shoot by swinging the turret over to the far left.

A sparkling line of fire raced across the belly of the Mangusta as Mugabe's HE rounds exploded harmlessly against the ship's belly armor. He had scored, but the rounds had not been able to punch through her heavily armored skin.

The burst had, however, spooked the Mangusta's pilot and he threw his machine out of Mojo's line of fire. As Wolff racked the Griffin around to try to get in behind his opponent, Mojo quickly switched the ammo feed over to supply AP, armor-piercing ammunition, to the gun. When the Mangusta snapped into his sights again, he triggered a short burst.

This time, he was on target and the chain gun did its job.

The AP rounds punched through the Mangusta's armor, tearing into the top of the canopy and smashing their way through to the rotor masthead. The Mangusta staggered in the air, mortally wounded. Slowly, the gunship nosed over and started for the ground.

As Wolff followed the Mangusta into the dive, Mugabe switched back to the HE ammunition for his chain gun and opened up again on the stricken machine as it plummeted for the ground. The 25mm HE shells ripped into the airframe before exploding. Large chunks of the chopper's skin and framing tore away to blow back in the slipstream. Greasy black smoke poured from both turbines and trailed back in the slipstream. The ship was fatally crippled, but Mojo did not take his fingers off the trigger.

More 25mm HE rounds tore into the Mangusta's turbine nacelles, sparkling as they detonated against the armor plating. Flickering fingers of flame appeared in the greasy black smoke pouring from the exhausts. The fingers of flame became a blaze as the fire engulfed one of the turbine nacelles. The doomed gunship's dive steepened as it headed directly for the famous "Hollywood" sign on the hill overlooking the freeway.

"Oh, shit!" Wolff said when he saw where the stricken chopper was going to hit.

For the briefest instant, the two flyers saw the Mangusta fly nose first into the sign and crumple into a ball. Then it exploded in a billowing ball of fire. Flaming debris and burning fuel flew up into the air and rained down on the tinder-dry dead vegetation surrounding the sign. The fire quickly spread, turning the rusting white letters of the sign to fire-blackened grays. Another renowned California landmark was going up in flames.

Wolff racked the Griffin into a tight spiraling turn low over the burning wreckage of the Mangusta. The greasy black smoke from the burning JP-4 almost obscured the wreck, but from what he could see, he knew that there would be no survivors in that inferno.

"Dragon Control," he keyed his throat mike. "This is Dragon One Zero."

"Control, go ahead."

"This is One Zero. Be advised that the last bandit has gone down in the last 'O' of 'Hollywood.'"

"This is Control," came Mom's puzzled voice. "Say again, please. I did not copy your last transmission."

Wolff grinned under his face mask as he keyed his throat mike. "This is Dragon One Zero. I say again. The last bandit has crashed into the 'Hollywood' sign on the hill overlooking tinseltown. The wreckage is lying in the last 'O' of the sign. There are no survivors, but we've got us a pretty good brush fire going down there."

There was a long pause. "Control copy."

"This is One Zero, we are returning to base."

"Control clear."

Wolff righted the Griffin and headed back to the airfield at three-quarters throttle. He had enjoyed just about all of Southern California that he could stand for one lifetime.

CHAPTER 29

Torrance Airfield, Los Angeles

Once on the ground, Wolff went directly into Buzz's office. "How's Legs?" he asked.

Buzz looked grim. "The hospital reports that she's okay physically, but she's not in too good shape psychologically. She got worked over pretty badly, and while it's hard for any woman to go through something like that, it was real bad for her."

Wolff understood that one very well. Sandra prided herself on being able to take care of herself under any circumstances, but this circumstance had been more than even she had been able to handle. This experience was bound to have shaken her belief in herself, and that was always a hard thing to deal with.

"When can we go and see her?"

"Some of the people are going this afternoon," Buzz replied.

"Good," Wolff smiled. "I'll tag along and see if I can take her mind off her troubles."

"I'm still wrapping this up," Buzz said, "so I can't make it this afternoon. Can you give her my regards?"

"I'll be glad to."

"Speaking of wrapping this up," Wolff said sarcastically.

215

"When does the shooting investigation board circus start working on Gunner?"

"There's not going to be a shooting investigation," Buzz said firmly.

Wolff looked at him. "Why not?"

"Because Gunner wasn't a cop when he wasted Miller," Buzz explained. "His resignation was valid."

"Well, I'll be damned," Wolff said softly.

"And," Buzz continued, "there isn't even going to be a grand jury investigation, either."

Now Wolff was really confused. "But he killed a police officer!"

Buzz smiled grimly. "He killed a criminal in a foreign country," he corrected Wolff. "Miller was not a cop when he was in Mexico because he was not down there on official duty. And, as far as the Federales are concerned, he was just another run-of-the-mill American citizen who was engaged in criminal activities."

"But aren't they going to hold Gunner for murder?"

Buzz shook his head. "He's already been released and sent back across the border."

When Wolff looked blank, Buzz went on to tell him the rest of the story. "It seems that there's a Mexican law dating back to the old Pancho Villa days that states that a law-abiding citizen has the right and, in fact, the obligation to try to keep a person from committing a criminal act. It's similar to our old Posse Comitatus laws. Anyway, as far as the Mexican authorities are concerned, Gunner was acting within his legal rights to take Miller down to keep him from killing Officer Revell."

"But he carved him to pieces," Wolff said. "He didn't simply kill him to stop a crime."

"The law doesn't care how the criminal is killed, only that he is."

"Jesus Christ," Wolff said softly, shaking his head.

"Where's Gunner now?"

"He's undergoing treatment for his wound," Buzz said. "And, as soon as he is released, he will be reinstated in the Tac Force at his previous rank."

"How in the hell did you manage that?" Wolff asked.

Buzz smiled. "Washington decided that they wanted to have him back on the force. It was either that or risk having the entire story show up on the front pages of every newspaper in the nation."

"I detect a little blackmail here," Wolff grinned.

"You're not the only manipulating bastard around here," Buzz said gruffly. "And you're not the only one who stands up for his people."

"Thanks, Buzz," Wolff said. "He's a good man. We need him."

"Tell me something I don't know," Buzz said. "Now you'd better get cleaned up if you're going to go see Legs."

"Yes, sir."

Sandra lay in the hospital bed and looked past the piles of flowers to stare out the window. Every flat surface in the room was piled high with flowers and get-well-quick cards from the men and women of Dragon Flight. The flowers didn't cheer her up, though. They reminded her too much of flowers in a funeral parlor.

"You decent?" came the husky but feminine voice from the door.

Sandra sat up. "Sure, Ruby. Come on in."

Mom walked into the room wearing her Class A TPF blue uniform complete with all of her hero buttons. "How're you doing, kid?"

"Fine," Sandra replied. "What's with the monkey suit? Is this an official visit?"

Ruby smiled. "No, this is personal and private. But the

heavy iron," she tapped the ribbons above the left breast pocket of her uniform tunic, "gets me past all the nurses and doctors."

Sandra laughed, but it sounded hollow to Ruby's ears.

She sat down on the edge of the bed and looked Sandra directly in the eyes. "Do you want to talk about it? Sometimes it helps."

Sandra shook her head vehemently. "No, Ruby, it's okay. Really it is. I'll survive, I mean, it's not like I'm the only woman who's ever been raped. I'll get over it."

Ruby looked out the window for a moment, her face expressionless. "You'll survive, that's true, but you won't forget what happened, I can promise you that."

She looked back at Sandra. "You've heard the story about my last street mission, haven't you?"

"I'm sure you have," Ruby continued, not giving Sandra time to answer. "It's firmly enshrined in the Tac Force mythology. Ruby Jenkins, tough girl cop, goes out, tracks down a drug gang, and gets the shit shot outta her. She almost dies, bravely recovers, and goes on to become Mom at Dragon Flight. You know the story."

Sandra nodded.

"Well, there's a little more to it than that." Ruby paused and took a deep breath. "I was shot killing the guy who raped me."

Sandra was stunned into silence for a long moment. "Ruby," she said softly. "I didn't know."

Mom smiled thinly. "Not too many people do, except Buzz and the people who keep my medical records. Now you do, too. I survived, but, believe me, I haven't forgotten it. And I don't think I ever will. I still dream about it, but not as often as I used to. It's true what they say about time healing wounds. But believe me, during those first few months I really didn't think I was going to make it."

She held out her wrists in front of her and Sandra could

make out the faint but unmistakable traces of razor cuts. Deep ones. Her eyes flew back up to Ruby's.

"Why?" was all she could say. It was almost a whisper.

"Because during those first few months I was just like you. I had bought into my own mythology. I thought that I was the toughest broad on the block. And, since I had gotten my revenge on the bastard who had raped me, I thought that I could survive anything. But I was dead wrong. I didn't realize just how deep the wounds really went. The psychological ones, I mean."

She reached out and took Sandra's hands. "The physical part isn't what really tortures a woman who's been raped. It's the realization that you were proven so vulnerable that starts eating away at you. And, knowing that the most private aspect of yourself can be so easily taken away and violated is one hard fucking thing to deal with."

She locked eyes with Sandra. "And, believe me, I know how hard it is. I didn't deal with it well and I cut my wrists, but that only made it worse."

It was Sandra's turn to comfort the older woman. "Ruby, I'm sorry," she said. "I didn't know."

Neither woman spoke for a few moments. The silence was broken by the sounds of Sandra crying. At first the sounds were muffled, but they started to increase as Sandra finally let go and the anger she had struggled to keep in check came boiling out of her.

"That goddamned bastard," she sobbed angrily. "That motherfucking son of a bitch, he had no right to do that to me. He had no goddamned right!"

Ruby reached over, took Sandra in her arms, and let her cry it out. As soon as Sandra's sobs subsided, Ruby released her.

"There's a bunch of people standing out there in the hall who want to come in here and see you," she said. "I know that you really don't want to see them right now, but they care about you and they're worried shitless. Why don't you let them come in and see that you're okay?"

Sandra was silent for a moment. "Okay," she sniffed. "But let me get fixed up first."

Ruby helped her wash her face, brush out her hair, and put on a little makeup.

"How do I look?" Sandra asked.

"Like shit." Ruby smiled as she stood up to go to the door. "But you'll do."

Everyone who filed into the small room was dressed in their Class A blues. Except, of course for Wolff. The pilot was wearing a faded pair of jeans, his beat-up, colorful World War II leather flying jacket, and his aviator shades. Everyone else was trying hard to hide their concern, but Wolff was wearing his usual big grin.

"Hi, Legs," he said brightly as he sauntered up to her bed. "I brought you something."

He dug into his pocket, brought out a brightly wrapped package with a big bow on the top and handed it to her. "Go on," he urged. "Open it."

She tore through the wrapping paper and lifted the lid of the box. Inside lay a square, thin piece of metal with rivet holes in all four corners. The printing on it was in a foreign language: Italian.

"It's the data plate off of one of those Mangustas," Wolff said proudly. "I nailed both of them and I wanted to share the trophies with you."

"But I didn't do anything."

"Oh yes you did," Wolff corrected her, his voice serious. "If it hadn't been for your report on their stealth capability, Mojo and I would have gotten our asses shot down for sure. As it was, we were able to change the radars to defeat their counter-measures. And, when we caught up with them, we blew them outta the sky. Thanks."

One after the other, the rest of the men and women of

Dragon Flight came up to Sandra, expressed their concerns, and talked for a moment before leaving.

Wolff hung behind as the others filed out. As soon as they had all left, he sat down on the edge of the bed. "How are you really doing?" he asked, his sincere concern very evident in his voice.

"I'm okay," she answered, touched by his concern. "I'm still a little battered and bruised, but they say I'll feel better tomorrow."

"Good," he grinned broadly. "How 'bout you and me going out for dinner as soon as you get outta here?"

Sandra smiled faintly. "Wolfman, you never quit, do you?"

Wolff shrugged, then grinned boyishly. "You didn't answer my question."

Sandra's smile grew. "You know I don't go out with the men I work with."

She paused for a moment. "But, since I don't fly with you, I will. But only under one condition," she added quickly.

"What's that?"

"I pick up the tab."

Wolff grinned from ear to ear. "I wouldn't have it any other way."

"You bastard."

ABOUT AUTHOR MICHAEL KASNER

Michael William Kasner was born in Pensacola Florida 11/17/1941. A Navy brat, by age fifteen, he had lived in more than 30 homes. The oldest of four children, his first interests were model airplanes and rockets, hot rods and reading. He grew up reading ancient Greek myths, military history, and science fiction. After his father's Navy retirement, the family moved to Blodgett, Oregon where he attended Eddyville High School and then Oregon State University.

Upon graduation from OSU in 1964, he received the honor of ROTC Student of the Year and accepted a commission in the active-duty U.S. Army. He served in the Army for 13 years rising to the rank of Captain. Michael's Army career included two tours of duty in Germany and two combat tours in Vietnam.

Profoundly interested in history and ancient civilizations, Michael spent a great deal of his life educating himself about how these societies regarded their warriors. While stationed in Worms and Mannheim, Germany, 1966 -1967, he made the first of many visits to Greece. There he toured Marathon and Thermopylae, the places where two of the greatest military battles in history took place.

His first tour of Vietnam, 1967-68, was in Nha Trang where he commanded a rapid-reaction platoon consisting of Nung ethnic Chinese mercenaries at Camp John F. McDermott. He then returned to the U.S. for advanced Special Forces training at Ft. Benning and Redstone Arsenal. During his second tour in

Vietnam, 1970-1971, he commanded "Echo" company 3rd Battalion 22nd Infantry division. Here he led a Mobile Strike Force Command or MIKE Force.

After Vietnam, Michael was stationed in Berlin, Germany, where he developed and opened a military museum dedicated to the history of the U.S. occupation of Berlin after World War II. In his spare time he enjoyed racing sports cars with clubs of American and British Army personnel. Cars were a life-long love of his, particularly British and German cars, his favorite being his Lotus Europas.

Michael was awarded the following: Bronze Star (2nd Oak Leaf Cluster); Air Medal; Army Commendation Medal; Army of Occupation Medal (Berlin); National Defense Service Medal; Vietnam Service Medal – Battle Stars: Vietnam Counteroffensive III, IV, V, VII, Tet Counteroffensive, Winter/Spring 1970 Counteroffensive, Sanctuary Counteroffensive; Republic of Vietnam Gallantry Cross Unit Citation with palm; Republic of Vietnam Campaign Medal; Qualifications: Combat Infantry Badge and Expert Infantry Badge.

Upon leaving the Army, he returned to Oregon and enrolled in the University of Oregon, receiving a M.A. in Art History with an emphasis on military art. His thesis entitled "A Proposed Reconstruction of the Weaponry of the 'Battle Relief' of the Alexander Sarcophagus" focused on ancient Greek weapons.

Michael planned a career as a museum curator, but discovered a talent for writing that re-directed his plans. After writing non-fiction articles for several military and sports car magazines, including Soldier of Fortune, he tried his hand at writing fiction, and his career as a writer of classic pulp fiction took off. He wrote war adventure, police adventure, and sci-fi adventure. He wrote about three novels a year, and he was pleased once at seeing a Danish translation of one of his books in an airport in Copenhagen. He wrote for a number of different series to include Black Ops, War Keep, Hatchet, and Chopper Cops. His biggest literary frustration was that he could not find an interested publisher for his 50th book -- in his mind, the definitive novel about ancient Greece. It is the story of a man who knows he will die in battle the next day. "In great attempts, it is glorious even to fail," he liked to say.

During his years as an author, Michael became very active in local historical re-enactment, founding Legio II Augusta, a Roman re-enactment group. He built a working, half-size Roman onager catapult and after finding a foundry that poured bronze, he started a business making replica weapons. That online business, Archaic Bronze, was just starting to take off at the time of his death.

His first marriage to Merrialyce von Krosigk ended in divorce. They had two children, Erika and Alexander Kasner. A second marriage to Monika Augurski, a woman he met and fell in love with in Germany, ended in 1983. Michael married for the third time in 1985; when he and Claudia Rosemont separated in 2003 they chose not to divorce and remained close.

Michael died of acute leukemia on March 19, 2008, at age 66. He was buried in Willamette National Cemetery in the uniform of a Roman tribunal soldier. He is survived by his widow, his children, his sister and youngest brother.

CALIBER COMICS GOES TO WAR!
HISTORICAL AND MILITARY THEMED GRAPHIC NOVELS

**WORLD WAR ONE:
MO MAN'S LAND**

ISBN: 9781635298123

*A look at World War 1 from
the French trenches as they
faced the Imperial German
Army.*

**CORTEZ AND THE FALL
OF THE AZTECS**

ISBN: 9781635299779

*Cortez battles the Aztecs
while in search of Inca
gold.*

**TROY:
AN EMPIRE UNDER SIEGE**

ISBN: 9781635298635

*Homer's famous The Iliad and
the Trojan War is given a
unique human perspective
rather than from the God's.*

WITNESS TO WAR

ISBN: 9781635299700

*WW2's Battle of the Bulge
is seen up close by an
embedded female war
reporter.*

THE LINCOLN BRIGADE

ISBN: 9781635298222

*American volunteers head
to Spain in the 1930s to
fight in their civil war
against the fascist regime.*

**EL CID:
THE CONQUEROR**

ISBN: 9780982654996

*Europe's greatest warrior
attempts to unify Spain
against invading foreign
and domestic armies.*

WINTER WAR

ISBN: 9780985749392

*At the outbreak of WW2
Finland fights against an
invading Soviet army.*

**ZULUNATION:
END OF EMPIRE**

ISBN: 9780941613415

*The global British Empire
and far-reaching influence
is threatened by a Zulu
uprising in southern Africa.*

AIR WARRIORS: WORLD WAR ONE #V1 - V4   *Take to the skies of WW1 as various fighter aces tell their harrowing stories.*
ISBN: 9781635297973 (V1), 9781635297980 (V2), 9781635297997 (V3), 9781635298000 (V4)

FROM AWARD-WINNING COMIC WRITER AND ARTIST
WAYNE VANSANT
COMES TALES FROM WORLD WAR II

An action/adventure tale of the French Legionnaire soldier, Battron, who is involved with the liberation of a freebooting French ship, the Martel, from a heavily guarded Vichy French port during WWII. The Allies want the ship destroyed; the Germans have sent serious resources and firepower to save it. But a critical security leak in British intelligence could jeopardize not only the mission but Battron's life. The key is the beautiful former mistress of the Martel's captain, enlisted in the hope she can convince him to join the Free French movement with his ship. But has she told the Allies all she knows? And can Battron and his skillful commandos complete their dangerous mission in time under the luming shadow of the pending Allied invasion of North Africa?

Collection of tales involving the German Waffen SS from acclaimed creator and comic artist Wayne Vansant. These stories deal with the German Panzer troops during World War II and collects the highly acclaimed Battle Group Peiper story, Witches' Cauldon saga, along with three short tales. Knights of the Skull covers the war experiences of young German troops on the Eastern Front to the massacre of American troops near Malmedy Belgium to the harsh conditions of a crushing winter and engagements against an unrelenting Soviet troop onslaught.

The epic and incredible telling of the early days of the United States during the Second World War. Days of Darkness covers the darkest days of WWII for the US, when the country went from the tragedy of Pearl Harbor to the triumph at Midway. Covering in detail is the attack of the US Naval base and the devastation of the fleet in Hawaii, then the action moves to the evacuation and fall of the Philippines to the horror of the Death March of Bataan, and finally to the dramatic Battle of Midway which stopped the Japanese juggernaut in the Pacific.

"Heavy on authenticity, compellingly written and beautifully drawn." - Comics Buyers Guide.

WWW.CALIBERCOMICS.COM

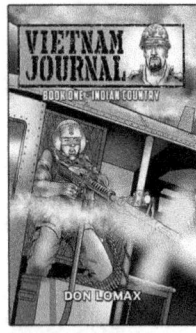

ALSO AVAILABLE FROM DON LOMAX

HIGH SHINING BRASS

High Shining Brass is based on the true story of an American spy during the Vietnam War as told to Don Lomax by agent Robert Durand who chronicles the tale. Durand was a member of a black-ops team, code- named "Shining Brass." The series depicts the horrific atrocities witnessed and performed by the once naïve special forces member as he attempts to perform his duties and understand the true meaning behind the madness. Durand's group was under the command of a combined force, comprised of every branch of the services, and headed up by the ever-popular Central Intelligence Committee. It's a journey into a shadow world of treachery and deceit—and reveals the way lives of Americans were traded about carelessly during the war in Vietnam.

ISBN: 978-1544962191 $14.99US

ABOVE AND BEYOND

Beginning in May of 2007, noted comic writer and illustrator Don Lomax teamed up with Police and Security News magazine to produce the series "Above and Beyond" - real life depictions of heroic acts by law enforcement professionals. Just as our soldiers here and abroad deserve recognition for their unwavering service, so do the men and women who protect and serve the citizens of the United States. Contained within these pages are just a few stories of these individuals who have demonstrated selfless bravery and heroic action under the most difficult circumstances and gone above and beyond the call of duty.

ISBN: 978-1635299601 $ 9.99 US

WWW.CALIBERCOMICS.COM

ALSO AVAILABLE FROM CALIBER COMICS

QUALITY GRAPHIC NOVELS TO ENTERTAIN

THE SEARCHERS: VOLUME 1
The Shape of Things to Come

Before *League of Extraordinary Gentlemen* there was *The Searchers*. At the dawn of the 20th Century the greatest literary adventurers from the minds of Wells, Doyle, Burroughs, and Haggard were created. All thought to be the work of pure fiction. However, a century later, the real-life descendents of those famous characters are recuited by the legendary Professor Challenger in order to save mankind's future. Series collected for the first time.

"Searchers is the comic book I have on the wall with a sign reading - 'Love books? Never read a comic? Try this one! ....money back guarantee..." - Dark Star Books.

WAR OF THE WORLDS: INFESTATION

Based on the H.G. Wells classic! The "Martian Invasion" has begun again and now mankind must fight for its very humanity. It happened slowly at first but by the third year, it seemed that the war was almost over... the war was almost lost.

"Writer Randy Zimmerman has a fine grasp of drama, and spins the various strands of the story into a coherent whole... imaginative and very gritty." - war-of-the-worlds.co.uk

HELSING: LEGACY BORN

From writer Gary Reed (Deadworld) and artists John Lowe (Captain America), Bruce McCorkindale (Godzilla). She was born into a legacy she wanted no part of and pushed into a battle recessed deep in the shadows of the night. Samantha Helsing is torn between two worlds...two allegiances...two families. The legacy of the Van Helsing family and their crusade against the "night creatures" comes to modern day with the most unlikely of all warriors.

"Congratulations on this masterpiece..." - Paul Dale Roberts, Compuserve Reviews

DEADWORLD

Before there was The Walking Dead there was Deadworld. Here is an introduction of the long running classic horror series, Deadworld, to a new audience! Considered by many to be the godfather of the original zombie comic with over 100 issues and graphic novels in print and over 1,000,000 copies sold, Deadworld ripped into the undead with intelligent zombies on a mission and a group of poor teens riding in a school bus desperately try to stay one step ahead of the sadistic, Harley-riding King Zombie. Death, mayhem, and a touch of supernatural evil made Deadworld a classic and now here's your chance to get into the story!

DAYS OF WRATH

Award winning comic writer & artist Wayne Vansant brings his gripping World War II saga of war in the Pacific to Guadalcanal and the Battle of Bloody Ridge. This is the powerful story of the long, vicious battle for Guadalcanal that occurred in 1942-43. When the U.S. Navy orders its outnumbered and out-gunned ships to run from the Japanese fleet, they abandon American troops on a bloody, battered island in the South Pacific.

"Heavy on authenticity, compellingly written and beautifully drawn." - Comics Buyers Guide

SHERLOCK HOLMES: THE CASE OF THE MISSING MARTIAN

Sherlock is called out of retirement to London in 1908 to solve a most baffling mystery: The British Museum is missing a specimen of a Martian from the failed invasion of 1899. Did it walk away on its own or did someone steal it?

Holmes ponders the facts and remembers his part in the war effort alongside Professor Challenger during the War of the Worlds invasion that was chronicled in H.G. Wells' classic novel.

Meanwhile, Doctor Watson has problems of his own when his wife steals a scalpel from his surgical tool kit and returns to her old stomping grounds of Whitechapel, the London

CALIBER PRESENTS

The original Caliber Presents anthology title was one of Caliber's inaugural releases and featured predominantly new creators, many of which went onto successful careers in the comics' industry. In this new version, Caliber Presents has expanded to graphic novel size and while still featuring new creators it also includes many established professional creators with new visions. Creators featured in this first issue include nominees and winners of some of the industry's major awards including the Eisner, Harvey, Xeric, Ghastly, Shel Dorf, Comic Monsters, and more.

LEGENDLORE

From Caliber Comics now comes the entire Realm and Legendlore saga as a set of volumes that collects the long running critically acclaimed series. In the vein of The Lord of The Rings and The Hobbit with elements of Game of Thrones and Dungeon and Dragons.

Four normal modern day teenagers are plunged into a world they thought only existed in novels and film. They are whisked away to a magical land where dragons roam the skies, orcs and hobgoblins terrorize travelers, where unicorns prance through the forest, and kingdoms wage war for dominance. It is a world where man is just one race, joining other races such as elves, trolls, dwarves, changelings, and the dreaded night creatures who steal the night.

TIME GRUNTS

What if Hitler's last great Super Weapon was – Time itself! A WWII/time travel adventure that can best be described as Band of Brothers meets Time Bandits.

October, 1944. Nazi fortunes appear bleaker by the day. But in the bowels of the Wenceslas Mines, a terrible threat has emerged . . . The Nazis have discovered the ability to conquer time itself with the help of a new ominous device!

Now a rag tag group of American GIs must stop this threat to the past, present, and future . . . While dealing with their own past, prejudices, and fears in the process.

CALIBER
COMICS

www.calibercomics.com